A Lot More than Love

A Lot More than Love

ADITYA PANDEY

Srishti
PUBLISHERS & DISTRIBUTORS

Srishti Publishers & Distributors
A unit of AJR Publishing LLP
212A, Peacock Lane
Shahpur Jat, New Delhi – 110 049
editorial@srishtipublishers.com

First published by
Srishti Publishers & Distributors in 2022

10 9 8 7 6 5 4 3 2 1

This is a work of fiction. The characters, places, organisations and events described in this book are either a work of the author's imagination or have been used fictitiously. Any resemblance to people, living or dead, places, events, communities or organisations is purely coincidental.

Dedicated to the lively spirit

of differently-abled people.

Acknowledgment

Well, here we are. Reading a dream come true. Thank you for grabbing a copy of this.

Starting the list with the first reader and the firm supporter of the author in making – Smita. Remembering our efforts of poorly editing the first draft will always make me laugh. I really appreciate you for encouraging me and for being there, always.

Coming to the motivation behind the book, my brother Amit Pandey. You deserve the best in life. Thank you very much for all your guidance. Special credits to my brother's friends for being the inspiration behind one of the main characters. You guys are legends!

I am grateful to my parents for always motivating me in this journey. It would have been impossible without your presence.

Special thanks to Dr R.H. Yadav for supporting me and my family in every aspect of our life.

My friends from B.E. – Rohan, Jayashree, Vaijayanti, Shraddha, Ashish, Pratik, Vinivesh, Ankita and others for bearing with me and my silly jokes. Yash, Karan, Abhishek, Huzefa for being the first buddies.

Many thanks to faculties and students at Somaiya and all my colleagues.

No thanks to Mithilesh, my useless childhood buddy, who is subconsciously part of every aspect of my life. I won't thank you!

Special mention of those relatives who found all my creative ideas meaningless and a waste of time. Sometimes I worked harder just to prove them wrong.

Thanks a lot to lord Hanuman for making this possible for me.

I am very grateful to my dear editors, Stuti and Vini for refining my story. Special credits to my publisher Arup, and everyone at Srishti for helping me to bring out this book in its best form.

Prologue

In Gorakh's voice

Ever thought of dying? Escaping from all your responsibilities and pain to become free from your burdens? I have felt it too!

Lying near the railway tracks, these thoughts roamed in my mind. I felt like crawling towards some running train and ending my suffering.

A few moments ago, I saw my life split into pieces when the train passed over my legs. Covered in my own blood, I was crying in pain and wanted to end it. But then, I thought about my mother. I knew she loved me a lot. My father would not want me to do this.

Then, I thought about Raj and Kairav. They would be devastated if something happened to me. I owed my life to them as well. So, I decided not to do it.

But I had already ruined Kairav's life and maybe, I deserved this. Perhaps now Kairav wouldn't care about me anymore. I knew that from now on, my life would be a nightmare. But even before this accident, my life wasn't really worth living.

I cannot recall even one incident when I made my parents proud. I shouldn't have chased Robert till here. Now I feel we should have listened to Panditji's prediction. He had warned the three of us – me, Raj and Kairav that bad things were going to happen. But, we ignored him.

I know you are wondering how the hell did I end up here! Let me start from the beginning, when things were pretty simple and I was just a regular boy, having a good time in life.

1

Results Out

Being tensed for the examination results is nothing new. It is indeed difficult to face the truth that you could not fulfil the expectations of your parents by scoring high marks.

Today was that fateful day in my life – my result day. Raj somehow became more irritating during such stressful situations. He kept messaging me till 3:00 a.m. and I kept comforting him, though I was more worried than he was. He had been a topper since my school days and I barely managed to pass. My friends called me Mr Perfectionist for securing average marks – mostly between 35% to 40%. It changed in tenth standard when I got 55%. Our twelfth standard results were going to be announced; the so-called results that were going to "decide our future".

My dad promised me that if I got more than 80%, he would buy me the latest mobile phone. It would have been a perfect gift.

I woke up at 7:00 a.m., too early for me on a holiday. Just then, my phone rang. It was my best friend Raj.

'Hello Gorakh, are you ready bhai? Remember we have to go to Siddhivinayak temple?'

'Yes, just wearing my shirt! I will see you in five minutes,' I lied, leaving my bed.

'Ok bhai, anyways I am ready. See you in five minutes,' he said and disconnected the call.

Raj was a sincere student who excelled in academics. In fact, he had topped the tenth standard exams. We were in the same school, but got different streams of study due to the difference between our percentages. Our fields changed; he chose science and commerce chose me.

My father had told me that it was simple to score 55% in tenth, also commonly called SSC. I could do it if I worked hard and focused on my studies. So, I studied earnestly with the topper. I cleared all my doubts and memorized everything.

But when I saw the question paper, I went completely blank. So, I did not have a lot of hope from my result. After all, I was just an average boy.

❖

Raj called for the twenty-seventh time, as my five minutes ticked to twenty. 'When will you learn the importance of time? Idiot! I have been calling you for the last fifteen minutes,' shouted Raj, glaring at me. Being called an idiot was nothing new to me since my dad always called me that.

Looking at my smile, he said, 'Now hurry up! Let's go. I know you will never change.' I followed his order like an obedient student.

'Kairav is also coming. He is bringing his car,' said Raj walking towards the Raheja compound.

'But yesterday he told us he won't be coming. He was going on and on about how praying won't change the outcome of our result. Then why this sudden change of plan?'

'He called me in the morning and said that it would be fun to watch us beg in the temple. He doesn't want to miss that,' chuckled Raj.

'Jerk! Sometimes he is overconfident.'

'Naah bhai, I don't think so. I am happy that he wasn't there in our school, otherwise I would have been a second ranker all those years,' said Raj, waving his hand at Kairav.

Kairav's life was so perfect that anybody would have been jealous of him. He belonged to a well-off Punjabi family. He needed no deal with god as he had everything sorted in his life. Raj wanted to be rich and smart like him and I just wanted to be smart. He lived in the Raheja compound, which was a few blocks away from our low-budget Ganganath chawl. We hugged him and sat in his SUV.

'You know what you wrote in the exam paper. Praying won't change anything, guys.' Kairav said and started driving. Kairav always said that he believed in god, but also believes that god won't be able to change anything for us. The fate of our life lies in our actions and thoughts, he often said.

'Not everyone is blessed with a brain like yours,' I taunted. 'Some people do believe in magic and good deeds of their previous lives.' Kairav laughed but Raj ignored both of us. He was very stressed out about the results.

❖

'Bappa, we are humans and we do commit mistakes, but please forgive us for that. Today is our result day. Bappa please, give us at least 90% marks and we promise to come and pray every Tuesday for one year.'

'Also, for the first five Tuesdays, we will come barefoot,' I added.

We were standing in front of lord Ganesha's idol to strike our deal. I secretly prayed only for 75%. Though Bappa didn't even give a signal through a falling flower as shown in old Bollywood movies, but in our hearts, we believed that our prayers were heard.

After we were done with our prayers, Raj said, 'Deal final! Now let's go.' Kairav was waiting for us outside after completing the *mukh darshan*.

'Which one of you promised that he would come barefoot if you get good marks?' joked Kairav. Raj pointed towards me and they laughed.

'*Jai ho Satvendra Babaji ki*!' said someone loudly and grabbed our attention. A man was lying on the ground with his forehead touching Babaji's feet. He stood up after a few seconds, touched Babaji's feet again, and left with a big smile on his face.

'Looks like Babaji is very knowledgeable. Did you guys notice how happy that man was? Should we also ask Babaji about our future? Maybe he will tell us some magical mantras that will solve all our problems,' I said.

'He won't tell us for free, Gorakh,' said Raj.

'Are you guys serious? You know how these babas are. They say general things that apply to everyone and yet, people think that baba knows everything,' said Kairav dragging both of us to his car.

'Jai ho Satvendra Babaji ki,' I shouted and Babaji looked towards us. He saw his potential customers going away and almost ran towards us.

'Wait bachcha! Where are you taking them? They look curious about their life. They have questions. Let me answer them,' said Babaji to Kairav.

'You can ask your questions as well and if you aren't satisfied, don't pay me,' he went on.

'Not interested, Baba,' said Kairav immediately. 'It's all stupid.'

'Please Kairav. It would be fun for you to watch us do stupid things,' I said.

'That's true,' he smirked. We walked towards Babaji's little shop beside a flower seller's outlet. Many chappals, shoes and sandals were lying near it. The flower seller kept an eye on the footwear of the devotees for attracting more customers. People used to come back after darshan, pay money for the flowers and take their footwear. A small trust-based system.

'Who wants to go first?' asked Babaji and Raj put Kairav's right hand in front of him.

'Tell me your birth date, time and place. I will make your *kundli* and match it with the palm reading,' said Babaji, taking out his mobile phone from the pocket. He entered Kairav's details in some android application. He read something in it and then looked at Kairav's palm. He used some kind of kundli-making app, I guess. He looked quite tense. After a few minutes, he said something that we should have taken more seriously and followed.

'Beta, you are very hardworking and will be very successful in your life.'

'I knew you would say something like this only. Typical response!' said Kairav, taking his palm back.

'I am not done yet,' said Babaji. 'Your kundli says that the people who you consider as your friends will be the reason for your doom. To live a happy life, you must stay away from them.'

'Whatever Baba,' laughed Kairav. We laughed with him.

'You are talking nonsense. They both are my childhood friends. They have relentlessly supported me during my toughest times.'

'I am not joking bachha. I am warning you. It's your wish whether you believe it or not,' said Babaji and signalled Raj to show his palm. He entered his details in the app and got more tensed.

'Beta, you tell me your date of birth as well,' said Babaji to me as he checked my palm. He did his readings and looked towards us.

'I know you people won't trust me, but your readings are similar to that of Kairav. You people can achieve big things in life, only if you stay away from each other. All three of you are unlucky for each other. You will lose everything and encounter near-death experiences if you remain together.'

'You are a liar. What's next? We will have to do some puja to avoid these problems? That puja will involve lots of money? We have heard about such scams before, Baba,' shouted Kairav.

'Give him his money. Let us leave, guys,' I said. I was terrified because I believed in astrology. I didn't show my fear to them.

'Why should we give him money? I was telling you guys that it is a bad idea. They are all scammers. The more you pay them, the more they will go on with their scams,' said Kairav.

'Why are they even allowed to sit outside temples? I am not giving him a single penny.'

'Calm down Kairav. Let's go,' said Raj.

'I don't need your money, bachcha. You will need it if you don't take my advice. All of you will suffer. I have never seen such a negative impact of someone on another person's life. Believe me and stay away from each other,' Babaji shouted, but we ignored him.

While coming back from the temple, a strange tension engulfed us. We were all affected by the Babaji's prediction, mostly me.

'Don't know about Kairav, but Gorakh, you are definitely unlucky for me,' said Raj.

'What? Why? You think Babaji was right?' I asked. My heart pounded.

'Yes, Gorakh. Remember we both went to buy a pair of sandals for me? That sandal's strap broke after three days.' Kairav laughed so loud that for a moment, he lost control of the car.

'Initially, I thought that the sandal was of bad quality, but now I know it was your ill luck, Gorakh,' laughed Raj. I hit him casually on his head.

'Ouch! See, you are causing me pain too,' said Raj. He deliberately cracked silly jokes to lighten the mood. Soon, the apprehension dissipated and it was replaced by our laughter.

❖

We reached home at around 10:30 a.m. and the results were to be announced at 11:00 a.m.. Kairav went home. Unlike Raj, I had a computer in my house. The result page wasn't loading. I reset the router but still, the page was not loading.

'Raj, check in your mobile,' I said.

'Already tried,' he said. He looked tensed, though I was confident that he would easily get above 80%.

'It's already 11:15,' Raj shouted.

'Don't shout bhai, I also know the time.'

I was worried and this suspense was killing me.

'Call Kairav. His internet is faster than yours,' Raj shouted again.

'Oh yes,' I replied and dialled Kairav's number.

'Hello, Kairav.'

'Hello Gorakh,' he said loudly due to the Punjabi song playing in the background. 'Today's party is fixed from my side for you both.' I understood that he had got good marks and he was celebrating.

'Oh great, but how much did you get?' I asked and put the phone on speaker.

'I got 96.58%.'

'Fuck you,' I responded without thinking.

'What?' he asked. 'I can't hear you properly due to the loud music.'

'Finally, you got the marks you deserved man. Congrats!'

'Thank you Gorakh, what's your score?' he asked.

'Bhai, the page is not loading here, Raj is also with me. Please check our results as well.'

'Okay, tell me the roll number,' he said. I told Raj's roll number first and put the phone on speaker.

'Congratulate him, he got 83.16%,' said Kairav. Raj smiled and closed his eyes, thanking Bappa with folded hands. I got scared. I didn't have a very good feeling about my performance. Hesitatingly, I asked Kairav to tell me my marks. He entered my seat number.

'Congrats bhai, you have also passed,' said Kairav.

'Kairav, tell me my percentage, please.'

'59%,' said Kairav in low a voice.

I immediately disconnected the call. I felt so ashamed that I wanted to disappear. Raj was quite happy with his marks, but he was feeling bad for me. He was considerate enough not to celebrate in front of me. I felt like the most stupid person on the planet.

'Don't be so sad, bhai,' said Raj, keeping his hand on my shoulder. You performed better than your SSC. I am proud of you. Don't worry! Marks do not matter in the long run.' I had heard this line plenty of times, but deep down, I knew that marks really mattered.

Raj belonged to a poor family, so they couldn't afford to have coaching classes for him. On the other hand, I went to the coaching classes, though it was not as popular as NARU'S classes where Kairav was studying.

Raj's dad worked in a plastic can-making factory on a very less salary. Even in such difficult conditions, Raj had managed to perform exceedingly well in his studies. He was very hardworking and I was an idiot. The fear of facing my father got to me and I ran towards the playground, away from home. Raj ran behind me.

Kairav was celebrating with his family. His dad had a big *kirana* shop which also had stationery items and a Xerox centre. For the smallest good news, his family was ready to party. What else would they do with so much money!

Raj and I were on the ground for an hour, and soon, Kairav joined us. They both forced me to go home and were trying to cheer me up. I wished they were in my place. To be honest, I wished I was in Kairav's place – rich and smart.

'Marks don't matter,' said Kairav putting his hand over my shoulder.

'I already said that,' whispered Raj.

'Oh! Don't worry, your dad will understand. We will come with you,' said Kairav confidently. He convinced me and I decided to go home.

My dad already knew my marks and was waiting for me. As I reached home, he pulled my hand, made me sit in front of him and shouted.

'Where were you? First, you get poor marks and let us down. Then, you disappear. You don't even have the courage to face us. What is all this?'

Though Kairav and Raj tried to explain and calm him down, my dad didn't listen. He gave me a two-hour-long lecture on the amount of money he had spent on my studies and the difficulties he faced in life.

He could have slapped me, but didn't, as my friends were present. I was very embarrased. Nothing could have gone worse than this.

❖

After getting scolded by my father, I went to the Chinese bhel corner. Kairav, Raj and I used to meet there. Kairav gave us a treat to celebrate his achievement. He planned for a party at a hotel, but we were content in our Chinese bhel. They tried to make me feel better, but I was deeply hurt. I was angry with myself.

'You geeks will never understand my pain,' I said.

'Let us go out tomorrow, let us have fun,' chuckled Kairav.

'The admission procedures will start soon. This is the time for us to enjoy and live in the present moment.'

Raj wanted to go, but was worried that he would have to spend money. I also wanted to go, but my marks were stopping me. I was now worried about my admissions.

'My dad won't allow me to go,' I said half-heartedly.

'You have to come, bhai. You can't change your past, but can surely have a fresh start,' said Kairav.

2

Mess at Marine Drive

Four days passed, but I wasn't able to seek permission from my dad for going out. Before I could say anything, he used to assign some task to me or would tell me to search for good colleges.

'The admission process starts next week. Bhai, we only have this week. Take permission somehow and let's enjoy tomorrow,' said Kairav. They tried to emotionally blackmail me into agreeing to their demands. I had no option but to give in. I realized that asking dad would be a foolish idea, so I decided to approach mom. I told her about the next day's plan and begged for permission. As expected, she was more compassionate.

She looked at me and said, 'Go dear! Enjoy your life. A lot of things happen in life. You have to learn from the misfortunes and prepare for the future. And don't worry, I will handle your dad,' she said, caressing my hair. I hugged my mom and thanked her. I called both Raj and Kairav and gave them the good news.

It was difficult for me to come, but it was much more challenging for Raj. His mother gave him fifty rupees and warned him that if his dad asks about money, he should say he got only twenty rupees. It was so unfair to Raj. He was a kind-hearted guy. He got good marks and deserved all the happiness in the world, but didn't have the money for it. I felt a bit ashamed again.

'Moms are so cool and loving,' said Kairav. He had no permission issues, even if he wanted to go to Goa or Bangkok.

❖

It was a Monday. We started at 10:00 a.m. Raj and I were waiting for Kairav and soon, he joined us. We caught the train for Chhatrapati Shivaji Maharaj Terminus (CSMT) and reached Marine Drive in an hour.

A cool breeze was flowing ceaselessly. It was as if we were in heaven or flying in the sky. It was a low-budget *Zindagi Na Milegi Dobara* moment for us. We went closer to the water. From start to end, its shore was accompanied by identical-shaped, big, and heavy rocks.

'What do these rocks look like?' I asked.

'These are tetrapods, bhai. When the roaring waves travel to this boundary of tetrapods, a part of its energy is absorbed by the rocks,' replied Kairav.

'My dad is a tetrapod too. He absorbs my energy all the time,' I said.

Marine Drive is one of the best places in Mumbai. It was blissful to go there in the evening, but we had to go in the morning since Kairav had plans with his family later in the day.

Once we reached there, we sat at the beach for an hour and soon, the photoshoot started with Kairav's iPhone. We clicked numerous photographs in different poses and expressions.

While we were having fun, we saw a group which had three girls and four boys. The girls were very attractive.

'I am going to propose to that girl in the red t-shirt. Let me go, please don't stop me, leave my hand,' said Raj, in an overtly dramatic manner. Kairav and I had our hands in our pockets.

'Please hold my hand! Stop me or I would propose to that girl.' To poke fun at him, we caught his hands and I said, 'Raj, please don't go. If that girl says yes to your proposal, what will happen to Bindiya? Don't cheat on her.' Kairav and I burst into laughter.

Bindiya was Raj's kindergarten girlfriend who stole his tiffin box and pencil box on their second date. He always became angry on hearing her name. Raj looked at us angrily and started chasing us. We were running and giggling. Suddenly, I stumbled and fell on the girl in the red t-shirt. For a while, she was beneath me and I was above her. She was beautiful and I was drowning in her seductive eyes. I never wanted that moment to end, but someone caught me by the collar. A guy from their group pulled me up. He punched me right on my face and I fell again.

'I have been watching you guys for half an hour. Earlier, you were staring at the girls, and now, you are intentionally doing tricks to touch them. I know guys like you very well,' he shouted. 'I will teach you a lesson.'

I stood up as he was going to punch me again, but Raj came in the middle and stopped him.

'Dude stop!' Raj said. 'How dare you punch my friend? We didn't do anything intentionally.'

Raj was a bit taller than me, but he wasn't very muscular and thus, he wasn't qualified to fight with that guy or even pass such comments. Soon, Raj realized that he had said something unwanted. The guy and his three friends surrounded us.

'Let's enjoy, the vacation is ending,' I teased imitating Kairav's voice. 'I was telling you that we shouldn't go anywhere, now see!'

'Shut up Gorakh! I have an idea,' whispered Kairav.

Suddenly, he pointed towards the girls who were standing at a distance and shouted, 'Hey girls, no guns please.'

I got scared. At that point, everyone including me, looked at those girls and they looked at each other. Kairav caught Raj and my hand and hushed, 'Run guys! There is no gun!' We got the cue and started running fast. Those guys were following us. They were fast and furious.

Soon enough, we caught a taxi and said to the taxi driver, 'Bhaiya, quick to the station.' We reached the station and caught the train. We all sat quietly as the train started. The moment of silence was broken by our animated laughter.

3

The Phone Call

The Marine Drive trip was one of the best and happiest moments of my life. We came back safe, which was enough for us.

I was busy playing GTAV on my computer when my phone rang. I paused my game to check who it was. It was Kairav.

'Hello, Kairav.'

'Gorakh,' said Kairav. His voice sounded low and heavy, as if he had been crying.

'What happened, bhai? Tell me! Are you crying?' I asked.

'Please come to my home Gorakh, bring Raj as well!'

'What happened? Hello, say something, Kairav!' I shouted at the phone but Kairav didn't reply and hung up.

I immediately took Raj with me and reached Kairav's house. It was surprising to see many people gathered there. We saw Kairav's dad sitting on the sofa. He looked worried and sick. He was surrounded by a few other Punjabi men. It looked like they were sympathizing with him.

We rushed to Kairav's room. The door was wide open. Kairav was sitting on the floor in one corner of the room. He was crying bitterly. A woman was sitting beside him, telling him not to worry. She wasn't his mom.

When he saw us, he stood up and hugged me. We got scared to see Kairav in this condition. He was the strongest and bravest amongst us. Upon asking multiple times, Kairav replied, 'My mom…my mom has been kidnapped.'

'What? When? How is this possible?' said Raj, losing his mind. A kidnapping was what we had heard of only in news or in television serials and movies. It had never happened with anyone we knew. It took a few seconds for me to process what Kairav had said.

'My mom had gone for buying vegetables and didn't return home. We called on her cell phone, but it was switched off. We called all her friends and tried to search for her everywhere, but we couldn't find her.'

We were shocked. Raj was on the brink of crying and I was still soaking in the information. Kairav continued, 'A few minutes ago, a person called on our landline and said that he had kidnapped my mother. He has threatened my dad that if he doesn't give him three crore rupees, he would kill my mom. He also said that if we inform the police, we should be ready for the consequences. He told us that he wants the money tomorrow, till then he will not harm my mother.'

Looking at the present condition we were clueless. We had never experienced anything like this. I wondered what it felt now to be in Kairav's position. He kept crying and we were unable to understand what to do.

'Everything will be alright, bhai. You are very strong. We will get out of this situation, I promise,' Raj wept.

Kairav also informed us that his dad could put together about two crores. He took one crore from his friends as loan. The kidnapper had called Singh uncle in the Gopli Fort at 2:00 p.m. Gopli Fort was a big garden that had many secluded spots.

'All our property has been kept on a mortgage for getting the money,' said Kairav. Guys tell me, what should I do? I can't understand anything.'

'First of all, stop crying bhai, everything will be fine,' I said, holding Kairav's hand. The statement sounded very formal, but that was the only thing I could think of at that moment.

'Should we try catching the kidnappers on our own? We will secretly enter the fort and catch them when they show up for taking the money,' said Raj, wiping his tears.

'What are you saying Raj? This is not a movie. We will give them all the money, I just want my mom back,' said Kairav. I gave Raj a stern look. It was clear from Kairav's condition that he couldn't be left alone. We wanted to support him in this tough time. We decided to stay in Kairav's house for the night.

❖

Raj managed to sleep for a few hours, but I was wide awake. I was tossing and turning. Sleep had evaded me. I couldn't stop thinking about the moments we had experienced a few hours ago.

Life loves to play games with people. It has the tendency to surprise by throwing unexpected obstacles at them. If time could be stopped, I would have stopped it at the moment when we were enjoying at Marine Drive. In a span of a few hours, our lives had changed dramatically.

I desperately wanted to help Kairav in saving his mother. Even if his father gave money to the kidnappers, there was no guarantee that they would leave Kairav's mom alive. And, if they left her unharmed, all the money would be gone and Kairav's family would become very poor and helpless. I knew Kairav did not deserve this. As his best friend, it was my duty to get him out of this quagmire.

Suddenly, I got an idea. I saw the watch which showed 5:00 a.m. I woke up Raj and told Kairav that we would be back soon.

Raj and I reached down the building and went towards the chawl, but I had to execute my idea. I told Raj to go ahead. The sleepyhead walked towards his house and I marched towards a PCO.

As I entered the PCO, my hands were shaking. It was difficult to take such a big decision on my own, but I was ready to do anything for Kairav's happiness. I entered a rupee in the telephone booth and called the police.

'Hello, Mumbai police, how can I help you?' asked the policeman.

'Hi sir, this is Gor…' I stopped myself from revealing my name. 'We need your help.'

'Can you please tell your name and where are you calling from? What is the problem?' inquired the policemen. I hesitated.

I should ask Kairav or his dad before telling the police. This isn't my decision to make.

I disconnected the call and sat down inside the booth. I felt helpless.

But they aren't in a stable state of mind. Once I succeed in my plan, they will understand why I did this. God, please show me the right path!

Suddenly the phone rang and I knew the policeman had called back. I picked up the call.

'Hey kid, are you okay? Where are you and what's the issue?'

'Shital Singh, the wife of Dhanraj Singh, has been kidnapped. The kidnappers have asked for three crores as ransom.

Mr Dhanraj will go to Gopli Killa to give it at around 2 p.m. They live near Sion station,' I said quickly.

'Who are you? Is this a prank?' shouted the policeman. I got scared.

'Please do not reach out to Mr Dhanraj as the kidnapper has threatened them to kill Mrs Shital if the police is involved. Please save her,' I said and hung up the phone.

I quickly ran away from the PCO to my home. I didn't know what would happen, but I did it for Kairav!

❖

Raj and I reached Kairav's flat by 8:00 a.m. He was miserable, so we tried our best to comfort him. In the meantime, we saw Kairav's dad leaving with two black bags containing the money. The kidnappers called on his cell and he instantly picked up.

'Yes, the amount is ready and I am coming. I have not informed the police, so please don't do anything to her.' Saying this, Kairav's father left to meet the kidnapper.

Few hours passed by, but we did not receive any information. We were waiting at Kairav's home impatiently. Kairav got more worried. Suddenly, the landline rang and he picked up the call instantly. It was his dad. We looked at Kairav's face to guess what had happened. I was waiting for the good news. I wanted the good old times to be back.

After a few minutes, Kairav dropped the phone and his face showed no expression. It was completely blank. He sat silently on the floor.

'This can't happen. I am dreaming. Yes… yes, I am dreaming. This can't be true.

'What happened bhai? We are with you, tell me what happened?' Raj asked, holding Kairav. I started shivering. Kairav didn't respond to Raj, rather he kept repeating, "This can't happen!"

At that moment, Raj's mom called him on his phone.

'Oh my god!' said Raj. 'Bhai, turn on the TV. See the news.'

I put on the news channel which flashed a breaking news.

'A lady has been murdered at the Gopli Fort. The police has confirmed that the name of the lady is Shital Singh who was kidnapped. As a ransom, the kidnappers asked for three crore rupees. They was planning to release her, but in the middle of the deal, they saw the police. As an act of defence, they killed Shital.

'The kidnappers also stabbed Mr Dhanraj Singh, Shital's husband, and tried running away. The police caught one of the kidnappers, but the other kidnapper escaped in a mini van. The police is still trying to find him. The escaped kidnapper took the ransom money and ran away. Mr Singh is admitted in Kantibehen Hospital.'

I could not believe what I had just heard. I felt ashamed and stunned. I had killed my friend's mother.

4

The Truth

We took Kairav to the hospital in a taxi. I was unable to think what to do. Guilty and unspeakable, I felt like jumping from the terrace of the hospital and killing myself. The only thought that was dominating my mind was that everything had gone out of control because of me. If I hadn't called the police, Kairav's mother would have been alive.

As soon as we reached the hospital, the doctor informed us that Singh uncle was out of danger. As Kairav saw his dad being carried out of the operation theatre, he went and hugged him.

'Papa, where is mom? Why did this happen to us?' sobbed Kairav. He wailed like a baby.

'I am with you, son. Don't worry, my tiger,' said his dad with teary eyes. He was on a stretcher. The ward boy pulled Kairav away from his dad. Then, he told us to let uncle rest. The guilt of being the reason for someone's death was eating me up from inside.

We make mistakes, but when someone else bears the consequences of our actions, it is more painful.

After a few days, Kairav got his father home. I didn't tell the truth to anyone, not even to my mom. Kairav told us that he wanted to be alone for a few days.

Two weeks passed, but Kairav didn't come for the night walk. Raj and I were sitting at the Chinese bhel corner.

'I feel so bad for Kairav. Although it's strange that police got to know about the kidnapping,' said Raj. I became restless and didn't respond.

Before Raj would have asked or said anything else, his mobile rang. It was Kairav. He told us to meet us on his terrace.

'Where are you people these days? No call. Nothing,' Kairav said as we reached there.

'You wanted space bhai, and told us not to reach out to you. So we waited,' said Raj and we hugged each other.

'How are you guys? What's going on brothers?' Kairav asked.

'We are good, Kairav. How are you holding up?' I asked.

'I am good. Soon, we all will live very close to each other,' said Kairav. His eyes filled with tears and a mild smile appeared on his face.

'What are you talking about, bhai?' asked Raj.

'We have to leave our house by tomorrow. We have nothing left,' he said. We knew that soon Kairav might have to vacate the house, but didn't understand why he said he had nothing left.

'Dad returned the one crore rupees he took from his friends by selling our lands in the village. And now, we are left with nothing. From tomorrow, we will be living in one of the houses in the chawl on rent. So, we will live closer to each other,' he smiled after saying this.

It seemed that despite all the painful episodes that happened in his life, he was happy that we would be together. But we knew he wasn't ready for this, both mentally and physically.

'Guys, I don't give a damn about money. I am ready to beg my whole life, but why did god take my mother away from me?

She meant everything to me,' he said, trying to hold his tears back, and failing miserably.

Raj broke down as well and hugged Kairav. I felt miserable. My heart got jammed and refused to pump blood. My inner voice said, 'Kick me bhai, I am the one who is responsible for the death of your mom, please punish me!' I felt like dying.

My body, heart and soul were forcing me to say the truth.

How could I be such a coward! If something happened because of me, I should have the courage to accept it.

This weight on my conscience was getting unbearable now.

'Kairav bhai, I am responsible for all this. I am the reason why aunty is not with us anymore,' I confessed.

'I don't understand, bhai. What are you saying?' Kairav asked, wiping his tears.

'I called the police and… and informed them that your mother has been kidnapped,' I said in a low tone. 'If I had not informed the police, aunty would have been alive.'

My eyes were closed while saying all this. I didn't dare to face the person who had lost his mother because of my foolish over-smartness. As I tried to open my eyes, I got punched on my face. I got two more punches on my stomach.

'You dog! You bastard! Who gave you the right to do all this? You are not a friend. You are a rascal. You ruined my life. I will kill you,' wept Kairav. He lost his balance and sat on the floor of the terrace. He screamed and cried aloud.

Finally, I cried as well. I tried to help Kairav to stand up, but he slapped and kicked me away. Raj supported Kairav to stand.

'Don't cry bhai, please, I beg you,' said Raj.

'I don't want to see his face for the rest of my life, Raj,' said Kairav, still sobbing. 'Tell him to go away or I might throw him off the terrace.'

'Calm down, bhai. Gorakh must have done this to ensure you could save both, aunty and the money. That's why he did it,' said Raj.

'Are you supporting this rascal? You both get lost from my life and leave me alone.'

He pushed Raj away. All of a sudden, he fainted. We picked him up and took him inside. As he woke up, he saw us standing outside his room. His first words were, 'Papa, tell both of them to get away from here. They should never try to talk to me again.'

We heard Kairav's last words for us. I knew that I had been foolish, but I only wanted Kairav's happiness. I hoped he would understand where I was coming from and forgive me someday.

5

A Beautiful Dream

In Kairav's voice

I knew I was privileged. I had everything a guy of my age would dream of – loyal friends, loving parents and money. And then, I lost all of these at once.

After leaving our lavish flat at the Raheja Apartment, we took a room on rent in a nearby chawl. We needed money, so I started looking for a job. My dad was on bed rest. On a Saturday evening, I went to the market to buy some vegetables. There was a lot of rush in the market, but things were cheaper here.

'Bhaiya, how much for the tomatoes?' I asked. He had three qualities of tomatoes priced at 120, 100, and 80 rupees, respectively. An aunty picked up the best tomatoes from the 120 rupees box and gave 100 rupees to the vendor for 1 kg.

'Give 20 rupees more,' said the vendor.

'No no. I bought it for 100 yesterday,' she replied and walked away.

'What do you want?' he asked me, a bit frustrated. I pointed towards the 80 rupees tomato box and told him to pick for me. Last time, I had tried choosing the best tomatoes, but half of them turned out to be rotten from inside. After buying every item on my list, I marched back home.

'Oye Punjabi boy, wait!' shouted someone from behind. I looked back but didn't find a familiar face. I was going to turn back, but then, I saw a girl in a red t-shirt and blue jeans waving her hands at me. As she came close, I read something written on her t-shirt, "Don't look at me". She was the same girl who had fallen because of Gorakh when he had gone to Marine Drive. She came running towards me.

'Well! Look who I found here. Hey girls, no guns, please. Nice trick you played that day,' she said, still panting.

'I am sorry for that. My friend, I mean Gorakh, didn't intentionally collide with you. It just happened,' I said, trying to escape from the situation.

'I know it wasn't intentional. I wanted to apologize for the way my friends behaved that day,' she said.

'It's okay then,' I replied and smiled a bit. 'I will leave now, I have some work.'

'You know I saw you from the other end of the market and then ran to catch up with you. Gosh, you walk fast.'

I didn't know what to say to that. 'Yes, yes I do walk fast,' I replied.

'Well then, see you,' she said while smiling and panting. I walked towards the chawl and looked back, she had her hands on her waist and was slowly walking away. She had indeed run to talk to me, but I wondered why she would do that.

❖

Two days later, I was at the market again.

'Here you are,' she said, tapping my shoulder.

'You scared me,' I said, holding my chest.

'Sorry. What a coincidence! We meet again,' she said.

'Yeah, true. Are you done with your shopping?'

'Yes,' she said, raising her cotton bag with a cheerful smile. 'You live nearby?'

'Ten minutes from here. Hey, I need to be somewhere. I need to go,' I said.

'Is something wrong? Am I not pretty?' she asked, coming a step closer to me.

'No, you are,' I said without thinking.

'Then, why do you seem so off?'

'What?' I asked. I was confused as to where the conversation was going.

'You know, at Marine Drive, I was observing you guys. You were playing like a kid, laughing, jumping, and enjoying every moment. You looked so happy, but now your eyes have so much pain. It seems you are running away from life. You look like a different person. Is everything alright?'

'You know nothing about me. You are just a stranger! Stop imagining my situation!' I shouted.

How can someone perceive me so correctly? I wondered. I was shocked and furious. I was so loud that people in the market started staring at us.

'It's okay,' she said with a bright smile. As if my shouting had just proved her point. I realized that I was wrong. The anger that came out wasn't hers to bear. Suddenly, I heard the sound of a cool breeze followed by rain. People started running to find shelter and I got pushed by someone.

Handling myself when I looked in front of me, she was gone.

❖

I needed to apologize to that girl, so I came to the market the next day, even though I had nothing to buy. She wasn't there. My heart became heavier

What was I becoming?

I came daily for a week to find her, but failed. I decided to look for her one last time and started taking the round of the whole market. Luckily, I saw her. She looked gorgeous in her pink salwar-kameez and was buying flowers from a hawker.

'Here you are,' I said, tapping her shoulder. She dropped her flower bag in surprise.

'Now you know how it feels,' I said while trying to smile.

'Very funny,' she said and walked away from me.

'Wait, I wanted to say something,' I said.

'I thought you don't talk to strangers,' she taunted.

'You were right that day,' I said. 'A lot has changed since Marine Drive.' She paused and looked back at me. 'That wasn't me.'

'Going through a rough phase, aren't you?' she said. I said nothing.

Breaking the silence, she said, 'Let's grab a coffee. There is a nice place a few minutes from here.'

We talked for hours that day. Her name was Sapna. She belonged to a rich family in Delhi. She wanted to try things on her own and thus, she came to Mumbai and lived in a rented apartment. She worked as a photographer for a magazine.

'I am sorry that you had to go through so much in such a short period. You must have wondered why all these things happened to you.' She again saw right through me.

What is with this girl?

'You aren't a bad person and these things have no logical explanation. I know that you didn't deserve this. But now you just need to stay strong for your dad and be the man that your mother wanted you to be,' she said, gently tapping my palm with hers.

'What do you think about Gorakh and Raj, weren't they wrong?' I asked.

She took a deep breath and said, 'Life isn't black and white, it's grey most of the time. It doesn't matter what I think about your friends and their decisions, you know them better. When the wound is fresh, the pain is at its peak and the vision is blurred with tears. It's difficult to see things clearly. Let the wound heal. Once the pain goes down, you will get more clarity.' Her words touched my heart and got etched in my mind.

The sun was going down, but we weren't ready to leave. We had five coffees each.

'Sir, should I bring one more coffee?' asked the waiter.

'No, We are leaving,' she replied. I didn't want to leave, though. We came out of the cafeteria.

'This wasn't a date, right?' I asked.

'No, it wasn't. Was it?'

'No, of course not!' I mumbled.

'We can be each other's go-to person. How does that sound?' she asked.

'It's perfect!' I smiled. Meeting her was like a beautiful dream. After all, she was a *khoobsurat Sapna*.

6

Admissions

In Raj's Voice

The process of college admissions was on in full swing. Gorakh and I were tensed and had to struggle a lot for securing the admissions. We went to every college for Gorakh's admission. As he had a lower percentage, it was difficult to find a good college that would accept him. Somehow, Gorakh managed to secure his admissions in a college nearby.

I was looking for an engineering college that had less fees but the average fees for one year were more than eighty-thousand rupees. I didn't have even five thousand in my hands, so engineering seemed to be out of my league. I secured a decent score of 142 out of 200 in the Common Entrance Test (CET). The marks were enough for admissions, but lack of money was stopping me from going forward with this. My mom also wanted me to do engineering.

Since childhood, I craved for many things which I didn't get. I wanted to fulfill all the needs and desires of my family and engineering would have helped me to achieve that. But I knew it was not possible for me, so I filled forms for graduation in science in colleges. My name appeared on the first list. I was going to take admission in the college, but my mom stopped me.

'You will not take admission in a B.Sc degree college. I want you to be big and rich. I want you to get all the things that I didn't get,' she said.

My mom was more courageous and determined than me. I decided that I will do engineering, no matter what.

❖

My mother forced my father to sell the land in the village. Ours was a joint family and my father's elder brother told us that the cost of the land was eight lakhs. It was decided that he would sell the land and would send our share of the money. We received four lakhs from that land, which was enough for my entire course. I entered my name into the engineering admission process. I decided that once I started earning, I would buy back that land.

Meanwhile, Gorakh's college started. He was pursuing B.Com and was the most stable among the three of us.

'Kairav has got a job now,' said Gorakh.

'What about his studies?' I said. Gorakh and I were sitting at the Chinese bhel corner.

'After he teaches tally and accounting courses in the morning classes, he works at a CA firm,' said Gorakh.

'Not sure what he is thinking about his career. The CA was a friend of Kairav's dad.'

Gorakh kept complete information about Kairav's life as he felt responsible for his condition. We knew that Kairav couldn't do engineering because of the high fees. Singh uncle was stabbed in the stomach so the doctor suggested that he shouldn't do any physical work. Thus, Kairav had to take responsibility, and he did. He never tried to talk to us. Once Gorakh had tried to stop him while Kairav was on his way to the classes. He wanted to apologize, but Kairav ignored Gorakh and walked away. Kairav even changed his number to break all ties.

My name appeared in a good engineering college and I filled its form. After two days, I had to submit the fee which was nearly Rs 85,620 only. The word "only" was written in the pamphlet of the college. It was "only" for the college but for me, it was more than my dad's annual income. I felt guilty that all our village land had to be sold for my education.

❖

'He is not picking up the call,' said my dad.

My uncle had told dad that he would be transferring the money to his account, but nothing as such happened. Uncle didn't pick up the call the next day as well. The last date passed, and I was unable to pay the fees. My admission application got cancelled.

To find out more, my dad took the train and went to the village. It turned out that my uncle had sold the land and kept the complete money with himself. He illegally transferred the house to his name, shattering all our dreams.

After my dad returned, he filed a court case on his brother, but property cases took a long time to end and that in no way would help me to get admission. My dad got really annoyed and blamed my mom, which made her cry the whole night. I realized that I had to do something to take charge of this situation.

'I will do engineering,' I said loudly 'Whatever happened will not change my destiny. The day I decided I want to be an engineer, I was completely determined to be one, and nothing can stop me from doing that.' My dad gave a stern look to me and my mom and then went to sleep.

Later, I went out for a walk with Gorakh.

'No money, no admissions, I will take a drop this year,' I said to Gorakh. I had already told to my dad I will not be studying this year and he had agreed. I thought of doing some job to gather money for getting admission into engineering next year.

'Take extra batches for tuitions,' suggested Gorakh. I started taking three batches for tuition for getting extra money.

7

A Ray of Hope

In Raj's voice

Ten months passed and still, there was no major development in our land court case. Dad visited the Lucknow court multiple times, but there was no conclusive resolution.

'Such cases run for a long time,' said my dad, taking a sip of the tea while reading a newspaper.

'I told you to forget engineering, but you, your mother and your foolish desires made everything worse. It's still not so late, beta. Take admission in B.Sc. It is a good course and you also have collected the money for the fees.

Taking tuitions thrice a day was a tedious job. I had collected forty-five thousand rupees in these months, but that was not enough for admission. Yet, I was adamant that I would do engineering and no other course. I also studied late at night for the CET exams to get a good score to secure admission in a good engineering college.

We came to know that Kairav had been promoted to the post of junior accountant. Though Kairav didn't consider us as his friends, but for us, he was part of our life. Gorakh knew almost everything happening in Kairav's life. Many times, we saw him with a girl who looked familiar to us, but we had no idea who she was.

I was very tensed about my future. I didn't want to waste my year again. We didn't get a loan from the bank so the finances were also not greatly managed. The work pressure and my apprehensions were overwhelming me.

'Go and bring milk from the market,' my mom said. Usually, mom preferred to go herself, but as I had not stepped out of the house for three days, she seemed worried. The admission day was coming closer and the thought of wasting one more year terrified me. I didn't feel like meeting anyone. But, mom forced me to go out and get some milk.

While I was moping towards the dairy, suddenly someone patted me from behind.

Curly hair, round face, huge spectacles – that was Nitin, my classmate from school. He greeted me with a warm smile.

'Hi Raj, how are you bhai?'.

'Fine and what about you?'

'I am good, bhai.'

He had a big bag on his back. The side pocket had a big black cylindrical container.

'What are you doing nowadays.' I asked.

'Engineering,' he replied. That single word acted like an arrow that pierced my heart. We studied together, I got more marks than him, and he was doing what I wanted to do.

'What about you bhai? What are you doing? You must be doing something better than me,' he said. Replying to it was even more painful.

'Nothing,' I replied with a fake smile. 'I took a drop and this year I will take admissions. I am studying for the CET examinations.'

'What? Why did you take a drop year? You scored more than me in the CET examination. You could have easily got admission in an engineering college? What more do you need?'

'Money,' I replied with teary eyes.

I told him everything that happened with me, which had forced me to drop a year.

'What did you do bhai? I feel so bad. Wish you had talked to me about this earlier,' he said.

'I didn't get you bhai.' He looked worried.

'You don't have money, but you want to pursue engineering! Just like you, there are thousands of such students who are facing the same problem. The government has a scheme for such students known as TFWS. Students whose parents' annual income is less than six lakh rupees can apply for this scheme by making an income certificate. For such students, the tuition fees in the total annual fees of the college will be waived off completely.'

'What does TFWS mean?' I asked eagerly.

'Tuition Fees Waiver Scheme,' he replied. 'In the total college fees, more than 90% is the tuition fees. Once, when you don't have to pay that, you can easily pursue engineering without any problem. You just have to do two things, first is to make the income certificate from the tahsildar office and second is to apply for the TFWS seat while filling the form.'

I felt god's presence in the form of Nitin. He showed me the way and promised to help out in the process. I hugged him tightly.

'I owe you bhai. What you did today for me, I cannot ever repay you,' I said.

He pushed me a bit and said, 'You will have to repay me, Raj. I will take three things in return.'

I had no idea that what he wanted but I was ready to give him everything.

'I want three things – first is a tea prepared by aunty, second is our lasting frienship and third is the treat that you will give me after you complete your engineering.'

8

Rejected

Nitin's advice ignited the fire within me. I decided to go to the tahsildar office after my entrance exams which were after three days. The exam consisted of four subjects – Physics, Chemistry, Biology and Mathematics.

I studied hard for three days and left no stone unturned to crack the examination. My efforts bore fruit as I was able to answer most of the questions. The examination went very well. Gorakh and I decided to go to Kulund to get the income tax certificate made the next day.

We reached the tahsildar office where we came to know that the income certificate (IC) related work is done only on Wednesdays and Thursdays. It was Monday so I had to wait for two more days.

On Wednesday, I went again, alone. There was an information desk where I asked about all the required documents. We had to make an affidavit. I went to the back of the tahsildar office because there was a court there. A large number of lawyers were present there. I asked one of them about the affidavit.

'Thousand rupees,' the lawyer said. I tried to negotiate.

'This is the minimum price for making the affidavit. Go and ask anyone here, they will tell you the same,' he replied. I had only four-hundred rupees, so I went to another lawyer.

'Five-hundred rupees,' he said. Then, I realized that there was no fixed cost.

'Sir, I have only two-hundred rupees. It is quite urgent, so please do it,' I said.

'Oh, it's urgent. I will do it.' The lawyer reluctantly agreed. He printed the affidavit and signed it and then, got the paper stamped by the notary. After I submitted all the required documents, the officers informed that it would take seven days for verifying them. After verifying it, they would send the affidavit, documents, and the IC form to another office. From that office, I would be informed about the next steps. I took the IC form and the affidavit and went home. On Thursday, I submitted all the documents to the office.

Now, I had to wait for seven days. Gorakh went to his industrial visit for a few days. Two days passed and I started feeling lonely again. I missed Kairav. He was on his own now. I felt the grief Kairav must be feeling, with no one to talk to, no one to share and no one to guide.

❖

The day finally arrived and I went to the other office which was located in Murla. I was expected to get my form and documents verified and also to be informed about the further procedure. When I entered, there was a small queue and I joined it. When my turn came, I showed them the token I had received from the tahsildar office. In the huge pile of forms, he started searching for mine. Fifteen minutes passed, but no luck. He asked me to help him. I checked all the bundles, but didn't find my form.

'Beta sometimes it happens. The paper gets delayed due to a large number of submissions,' said the officer. 'Don't worry, come next week; you will surely receive your papers.'

I went over the next week and the same thing happened. My documents were not in the Murla office. The officer suggested me to go back to the tahsildar office and check whether the documents were sent from there or not.

It was Friday, so I had to wait for five more days. After ten days, the entrance exam results were also going to be announced. The admission process was supposed to start after that.

Gorakh came back from his industrial visit. He got worried after listening to my situation.

'Don't worry champ. God knows how hard you have worked. You deserve everything. Mark my words bhai, everything will be fine, I promise. I am with you, bro,' said Gorakh.

We both went to the tahsildar office. A small queue was waiting for us again, but as the admissions were near, the initial document submission line was three times longer than the last time I was here. After waiting for a while, my turn came.

'Oh! It's really bad to hear that the documents didn't reach there. Few documents were left here due to some misplacements. Today, we sent those documents to Murla, so have a look there,' the officer said.

My CET results were out and I got 152 marks out of 200. I felt happy and as Gorakh had said, I hoped everything would be fine.

The admission process had also started. In the online form, I had to choose whether to opt for a TFWS seat or the regular seat. I opted for TFWS. Before admissions, there was a verification of all the previous mark sheets and the income certificate for those who opted for TFWS. The checking took place in some bigger government colleges.

'The mark sheets and IC checking in the college was supposed to happen soon, so I had to go to Murla again.

Gorakh and I left for the Murla office. I was very tensed. We reached the office. The person there recognized my face and started checking for my form and documents.

'Your name is Raj, right?' he said.

'Yes, I am Raj,' I replied. I became very happy.

'No, wait it's not Raj. It's Raju.' This statement changed my happiness into deep sorrow.

'Don't you know how to even read a name properly!' said Gorakh. He was very angry as he saw my face. He knew how much I was suffering.

'How dare you talk to me like that! Wait right there!' said the officer and ran to catch him.

'Illiterate jokers,' said Gorakh while running, looking at the officers. He quickly disappeared. If it was Kairav in Gorakh's place, he would have fought with the officers. They didn't know that he was with me.

I left the office as my papers were not there. Gorakh met me at the Murla station. I thanked Gorakh for saying what I should have said to them. We decided to go to the tahsildar office from there.

When we reached the office, the officer informed, 'Working time over, come next week!'

'Fuck,' I said unknowingly, but the officer didn't hear that. I started crying loudly as I could see my second year being wasted. The officer saw me crying. He came and took me inside with him. Gorakh followed. I told him about my documents which were missing for more than a month. He told us to go to room no. 207 in the same building. I raced there with Gorakh.

We reached the room but the thing written on the door was enough to shatter my heart.

"REJECTED TFWS APPLICATIONS"

I sat outside the room and Gorakh went inside. I was completely frozen and lost all my senses. Tears rolled down my cheeks. Gorakh came out after ten minutes.

'Bhai, they rejected your form. Our locality does not come under their list of localities for which they make IC,' said Gorakh. 'They could have told us this on the first day. The front page of your form has the address filled up. At least, they could have told this the second time when you came here. I wish I could kill them. How irresponsible?' Gorakh was furious but I had no energy left within me.

'The officer told me that our locality fell under the Old Dangoba House Tahsildar office,' said Gorakh.

I reached home and decided to give up on my dream of pursuing engineering. My mother cried when I told her about my decision, but I had no choice.

9
An Unexpected Call

In Gorakh's voice

I felt very annoyed as I was unable to help my friend. I woke up early and went to Raj's house, but he was not there. His mother had no idea where he was, so she told me to find him. I went to the ground. Finally, I saw Raj behind one of the taxis which were parked there.

'What are you doing here bhai? Let's go to the Dangoba house. Let's see what can be done,' I said.

'No, we are not going anywhere.'

He had given up, but I refused to surrender. I don't know why, but I had a feeling that it would be beneficial if we would go to the Dangoba House Tahsildar office. He refused to go but I packed all his documents in his bag and dragged him with me.

We reached Dangoba House and enquired at the help desk.

'It will take at least fifteen days to make the income certificate after the submission of the form,' said the man at the help desk. Raj behaved as if he knew what the person was going to say. We went inside and saw two queues, one for the submission of the form and the other, for the collection of the income certificate. "Show tokens first" was written in bold letters at the reception counter. All the students were standing in the queue which was very long. Raj had to submit his income certificate the next day. My hopes were also dwindling. Slowly, we started moving out.

Raj acted like a walking statue. He was lost in the ocean of sorrow. Just then, his phone rang. It was an unknown number. He disconnected the call, but the person called again.

'Pick it up,' I said and he did. Soon I saw a strange emotion on his face.

'What happened bhai? Who called you?' I asked. Raj had a smile on his face and tears in his eyes. He looked overwhelmed and was taking heavy breaths. I offered him some water to calm him down and asked, 'Can you please tell me?'

'It was the clerk from the tahsildar's office. He said that the officer of Kulund's tahsildar office called him to inform that he would get my income certificate made in a day. He felt guilty of the fact that the form got delayed due to his mistake. The clerk wanted me to come near the tahsildar's cabin with the application form and documents,' said Raj.

At Dangoba House, the procedure was completely different. Here, the affidavit was not required and the documents were verified in the office itself. Raj was thrilled to see the turn of events. We ran towards the tahsildar's room. The clerk was waiting for us outside. Raj gave the documents and the clerk told us to come over the next day.

Raj breathed a sigh of relief and he hugged me tightly.

'You always said that everything is going to be okay and it happened. Thank you so much Gorakh.'

❖

Raj and I went together the next day. It was 10 a.m. and the clerk was standing outside the tahsildar's room. Finally, he gave us the income certificate (IC). Raj held the IC very carefully in his hands, as if it was a one crore cheque.

From there, we directly went to the college where Raj had to submit an attested photocopy of all his documents. Raj got admission to the J.K. Institute of Engineering. He chose the branch Electronics and Telecommunication.

Once all the admission processes were over, Raj gave me a pizza party as it was the happiest day of his life. On that day, we missed Kairav a lot. After so many twists and turns, Raj had finally got admission into his dream course. My college had already started. Raj's college was starting after ten days as the complete admission process was still not over.

I was enjoying my college days, but my guilt never left me. It kept haunting me. No matter how much I tried, my past always spread its roots in my present.

10

Lone Wolf

In Kairav's voice

After working hard relentlessly for three years, I got a second promotion. Things were improving for us.

I had bought a house in the chawl now. My dad had gone to the village, so I lived there alone. Being alone in a house and managing everything on my own was never easy for me, but I persisted. Often, my mind wandered to old times when my life was simpler. I reminisced the beautiful memories where my mother cooked delicious food and appreciated me when I performed well in my studies. I longed for the carefree days which I spent with Raj and Gorakh. During difficult times, Sapna became my anchor who kept me sane all these years. She kept the hope within me alive.

I knew Gorakh followed me sometimes, but I didn't feel like talking to him. Every aspect of my life had changed because of his unwanted interference. He had made my life miserable. Even Raj had supported him, not thinking for a moment that I needed him. I always thought of Raj as my younger brother as I supported him many times. But when I needed him, he had chosen Gorakh.

Despite all this anger, I was happy that Raj got admission into an engineering college. I saw them eating pizza and I understood that it was a party given by Raj for his admission. The fact that he reached from vada pav to pizza must have made it tastier for Gorakh.

Now Raj must be in the third year of his engineering and Gorakh had already completed his graduation. Recently I met a school friend and from him, I came to know that Gorakh was planning to do Chartered Accountancy(CA) course. I also wanted to pursue my education. But now, my focus was money.

Lost in time, I saw the wall clock. It showed 1:30 a.m. Suddenly, my mobile rang.

'You are still awake,' shouted Sapna on the call. 'How many times have I told you to not get lost in thoughts of the past, especially at night? Go to sleep or else I will come and break your head.'

'How did you know that I am awake?'

'I woke up for having some water and randomly checked your "last seen" on WhatsApp,' she replied.

'Well, I was thinking about you.... I mean, I was thinking about giving a party to you,' I said.

'I know you, Kairav. Anyway, where should I come, Mr Senior Accountant?'

'Come to my place for dinner, I am cooking,' I chuckled.

'*You* are cooking, it's gonna be really bad. See ya lad, now sleep,' she said. Technically, we were still each other's go-to person, but I had fallen in love with her long back. I was scared to tell her as I didn't want to lose her.

❖

Sapna came with two bottles of beer. She said that she would need it after eating the food I had cooked.

'It's better than the last time. You really cooked this?' she asked.

'I have been practising,' I said.

'I had told you about Krishna, my assistant, right?' Krishna was an assistant photographer with the same magazine that Sapna worked with. He often hit on her and Sapna knew that he liked her.

'Yes, that ugly photographer, I remember.'

'I never said that,' she chuckled. 'Well, he finally mustered the courage and asked me out.' I stopped chewing for a second and then, asked her casually, 'And what did you say?'

'I said yes.'

'You said yes?'

'Why wouldn't I? It's not like I am seeing someone. I am excited to see how it goes.' I pretended that I was eating, but wasn't able to swallow the food. I wanted to tell her that I loved her. Suddenly I choked and started coughing. I wasn't able to breathe. I hit my chest, but it didn't stop. I stood up.

'What happened?' Sapna shouted and came to my side of the dinner table with a glass of water. I was still coughing. I felt like I would die. She understood what was going on. I was choking on food. She placed her arms around my waist from behind and bent me forward. Then, she started giving abdominal thrusts. After a few attempts, the piece of bread came out of my mouth. I gently laid down on the floor while she was continuously massaging my chest sitting beside me. I mumbled something but wasn't loud enough.

'What are you trying to say?' she said with tears in her eyes. I signaled her to come closer. She leaned forward.

'You,' I coughed. 'You have me. I love you Sapna. Please don't leave me now. No one will love you more than me.'

'You could have said that without choking and making me worried,' she said and sat on my stomach.

'How can I accept Krishna's proposal when you have been in my heart for year!'

'You lied....you...' I tried to say something, but she leaned on me and silenced me with a kiss. I kissed her back. I wanted to do it from a very long time. We kissed for a few minutes and then, my hands slid beneath her white t-shirt. I pulled her towards me and moved her beneath me. We looked into each other's eyes for a moment before I quickly helped her remove her t-shirt. I kissed her lips, her cheeks and her neck. My hands were moving all over her body.

'You won't remove your shirt!' she said and laughed, unhooking her bra. I followed her commands and we had the best time together.

❖

It was 1:00 a.m. and Sapna had fallen asleep. Or at least I thought so.

'Lost in thoughts again?' she said, keeping her hand on my chest.

'I will sleep now,' I said.

'You don't have to. Today, we will resolve it permanently.' She took out the beer bottles from the refrigerator and opened them. 'Here, take it! Tell me, what you are thinking.' She took a sip from her bottle.

'About the past, about my childhood, about the memories with my mom, Raj and Gorakh. You know, I forgave Gorakh for what happened to me long back.'

'You did? But why?'

'I thought about it a lot. I had thought of calling the police myself that day. I knew that we couldn't trust the words of the criminals. But I didn't have the courage, and somewhere, I was lost in the love of my mom. He should have asked me before making that decision. I wouldn't have listened to him, but he should have asked. He made a mistake but deep down, I know he meant well for me.'

'So why don't you talk to them again?'

'Because I forgave him for what happened to me after I lost my mom. But how can I forgive him for her death? It's not my place to forgive him. That place belonged to my mom as the tragedy happened with her,' I said as tears rolled down my eyes.

'Hey, stop crying,' she said. 'You know that your mom would have forgiven him, right?' I heard what she said, but I fell asleep. The beer had finally kicked in.

❖

'Kairav...Kairav *puttar*,' said someone. I knew the voice. I was trying to wake up, but my eyes weren't opening.

'Puttar, open your eyes.' I knew it was my mom. I succeeded in waking up.

'Maa, it's you,' I jumped off my bed and hugged her. 'I missed you maa. This world is lonely without you. I feel so empty. Now that you are here, I won't let you out of my sight.'

'I didn't miss you beta, because I am always watching over you. Every decision you take, every choice you make, I am in them. I am with you son,' she said, caressing my hair.

'Why don't you visit me then? I cannot see you as you see me.'

'Because I know you are capable of handling everything. You are a grown-up boy now.'

'No matter how old I get, I will always need my mother.' I kissed her cheek.

'I am here today to resolve your dilemma regarding your friendship.' I left her and sat on the bed. I knew what she was talking about. She came and sat beside me.

'You wanted to know if I forgave Gorakh, right? I forgave him puttar. He did what he thought was right for us. He didn't know what the outcome would be! And then, he confessed the truth. He apologized and yet, you banished him from your life. Even though you shunned him, he kept following you to ensure that you are doing fine. This kind of loyalty is commendable. He is like my son and I forgive him. It's time that you do the same before it's too late.'

She started fading in bright light. I tried to get a hold of her, but she was gone in a jiffy.

'Maaa, maa wait,' I shouted, waking up from the dream.

'Are you fine Kairav? Was it a bad dream?' asked Sapna as she woke up.

'Naah, it was the best dream of my life,' I replied. 'How can I see a bad dream when my dream girl is beside me.' I was still able to feel my mom's hug. I told Sapna about the dream.

'Your mom's blessings are with you baby. So, are you going to talk to them now?' Sapna asked with her head on my chest.

'I will, once I am back from the company audit,' I said. Our team was going to a company in Gujarat for its auditing. It was a fifteen-days work and I had to leave in an hour.

I was excited that the three of us would be back together soon. I decided that meeting them would be the first thing I would do, once I was back.

11

A Normal Day

In Raj's voice

'Wake up beta,' said my mom. I listened to her but refused to wake up.

'Poha is ready, who wants to eat it?' she said.

Poha was my favourite, so I quickly woke up. The lectures were for more than eight hours a day. The only good thing was the weekend break. I was really enjoying my college life since I was in my dream course.

I was in my third year and my daily routine had been the same for more than two years. I used to wake up at 7:00 a.m., eat breakfast, get ready, catch the train, and reach college around 8:45 a.m. I left the bed and went to take a bath, planning and thinking about the assignments I had to submit that day. My dad had also changed a lot in these years. He became more caring and supportive after my admission.

❖

'Two Chinese bhel please,' said Gorakh to the shopkeeper. The three of us had promised that no matter what, we will always meet at the Chinese bhel corner every evening. Kairav wasn't present, but we always came to the corner and discussed our life issues. Gorakh had already finished his B.Com and was planning to do CA.

'Do you think I can become a CA?' he asked.

'Firm determination and—' I was saying something but he interrupted me and said 'Just tell me what do you think? Don't repeat your old dialogues again and again.'

'Yes, you can. Because I am with you,' I said with a smile.

'I will work hard for it,' he said.

'Think about this, I will become an engineer and you will become a CA, it will be so interesting. I can request you to handle my accounts in the future,' I said proudly.

'Kairav's promotion, I told you about that right?' asked Gorakh.

'Yes, bhai. Any new information, agent Gorakh?' I asked.

'No captain,' he replied, eating his bhel.

'I have to pay the admission fees at the CA Institution and only then my name will be registered. After that, I will get the books,' said Gorakh. 'I will go and pay the fees tomorrow.'

Gorakh secured 70% in his third year and so he directly had to give the IPCC exams and work under a CA for three years. Once he cleared the two IPCC exams, he would become a CA. Lakhs of students try every year, but very few clear this tough examination.

❖

The next day, I was attending the integrated circuit lecture but my mind was somewhere else. I was speculating whether a CA earns more than an engineer. Suddenly the lecturer threw a piece of chalk which hit my head. Mr Pranab Goswami had a habit of hitting students with chalk when they didn't concentrate on the lecture.

'Tell me the difference between active filters and passive filters,' he asked me.

I had an idea about it, but was unable to recollect at that moment. So, I said, 'Sir, active filters are actively active while passive filters are passively passive.'

The whole class laughed, but Mr Goswami didn't find it funny.

'What's your number?' he asked.

'Sir, 99672—'

'Your roll number,' he grunted. I heard people laughing again.

'14, sir,' I replied. He canceled my attendance and threw me out of the class.

Since the professor had anyway sent me out, I decided to sit inside the college canteen. When I checked my WhatsApp, it had 456 messages.

Initially, I was shocked, but after checking the messages I came to know that there was a committee meeting at the auditorium. The committee name was Robolearn and in this committee, we could get to know how robots work and how their parts were made. There were seven committees in college and students could become a member of any committee of their choice. These committees arranged college functions all through the year and at the end of the year, provided certificates and 25% attendance to the members for their hard work and participation.

I went to the auditorium and saw that the meeting had already started. As I entered, the head of the committee stopped me. He was a final-year student, Gaurav Singh.

'Why are you late?' he asked.

'Sorry, I didn't see the messages,' I said. He didn't say anything else so I went and grabbed a seat at the back. I was not able to dedicate much time to the committee activities. They undertook seminars and other works and thus, kept calling the members for help.

I was the secretary of the committee. I hosted two seminars in the beginning, but later on, I decided to focus on lectures and practicals as the preparations took a lot of time.

The meeting took two hours to finish and it was decided that there was going to be an inter-college seminar after two months in our college. In this seminar, students from other colleges who are members of Robolearn would also come. The seminar was going to be undertaken by Dr Govind Lal Batta. He was a well-known scientist who built India's most high-tech robots. He was going to share his views and also select a few students as his interns to guide them for their projects. I felt excited and decided to work for this seminar.

Later at night, I met Gorakh. He had got his IPCC books after paying the fees. I was happy that after all these years, finally, the three of us had some clarity in life. Little did we know that destiny had other plans as everything was going to change for us forever.

12

The Poor Guy

In Gorakh's voice

Earlier, I didn't like books. But now, I got around thirty books which weighed more than twenty kilos.

I decided to be a CA so I had to immerse myself into these books to crack one of the toughest exam. The CA institution had their orientation program, for which I paid four thousand rupees and also a hundred hours of Information Technology Training (ITT) which cost me another three-and-a-half grand. Both training and programme had to be completed before joining the final course.

The five-day orientation program ended and my ITT training started. I had to wait for six more days to get it done with. All over, I had invested eighteen thousand rupees for my registration for CA, so now there was no looking back. Raj was also busy in his Robolearn seminar organization.

I decided to join some classes for the IPCC exams. I thought of registering for the classes after ITT training.

'Finally, tomorrow is the last day of my ITT training. Then, I just have to give the ITT exams. After that, I will peacefully prepare for IPCC,' I said to Raj.

'Oh, awesome bhai, but before IPCC exams, you have to do an internship for a few months under a CA, right?' Raj said.

'I have found a CA and have already mailed my resume to him. I am sure he will appoint me,' I said.

'That's a good plan, bhai. I am waiting to eat Chinese bhel with a CA,' Raj said with a smile. I smiled back and paid for the bhel.

❖

I packed my bag to go for the ITT class.

'Take care, son,' my mom said as I touched her feet. The moment I decided to pursue CA, I knew that hard work and dedication must be my default setting.

Raj was waiting for me. We used to go out of the house at the same time. The bus stop and the railway station were close to each other, so we walked together till we reached the bus stop. From there, Raj used to go to the railway station as he had to catch the train for his college.

'Hi, donkey,' said Raj as soon as I reached near him.

'Hi, Bindiya,' I said and then, ran from there as I knew Raj got angry whenever someone took her name. He ran behind me, but was unable to catch me as I always ran faster than him. I always won the racing competitions and Raj came second during school days. But my dad wanted marks, and Raj always got it more than me.

We both stopped running as we saw Kairav. We had seen him many times in these past three years as our timings matched. We even tried talking to him a few times, but he always ignored us. This time, instead of walking away, he stood and looked at us. We walked towards him.

'Kairav, bhai, what happened? Are you fine?' asked Raj.

'Yes, I am fine. I am better than I was in the last few years,' he said. Raj and I were surprised. In all these years, this was the first time he was talking to us properly.

'I have something very important to tell you guys,' he said, looking towards me. 'Let's meet tonight at the Chinese bhel corner and talk.'

'If it's important then let's talk now bhai,' I said.

'No Gorakh. You guys carry on. I am also tired. Let's meet tonight,' he insisted. We knew that he had just come back from a trip and I didn't want to lose this magical opportunity, so I agreed.

'See you at the bhel corner then,' said Raj. Kairav nodded with a smile and walked away. We were unable to believe that Kairav was willing to talk to us. We were excited for the night.

We were getting late and thus, Raj went to the railway station and I came to the bus stop. Usually, I had to wait for the bus for more than an hour, but on that day, I was quite lucky. The bus came within five minutes. I caught the bus, but there was no seat at the back. So, I had to move forward to find a seat. I did find a seat where I sat quietly, listening to melodious songs on my earphones.

Suddenly I heard someone saying, 'Stand up, this is a ladies' seat.'

Startled, I stood up and moved back towards the unreserved seats. I was curious to know what Kairav wanted to talk to us about.

Has he forgiven me? Or is he planning to move to some other part of the country, hence he wants to talk to us for one last time?

Lost in my thoughts, I looked outside the window. Suddenly, I saw someone on the footpath who looked familiar.

When I realized who it was, I freaked out. He was *the kidnapper*, the killer of Kairav's mom. He was the person who had ruined my friend's life and broken our friendship. He was wearing a muffler and a monkey cap to hide his face so that no one could recognize him.

'Stop the bus!' I said to the conductor. 'It's very urgent, please stop.'

'Stop, stop,' said the conductor to the driver and pulled the thread.

As the bus stopped, I jumped out and ran towards Robert. I shouldn't have run towards him, because he noticed me. He didn't know who I was, but he started running away. The chase started. I was happy that I had found him. I thought that if Robert would get caught because of me, Kairav would forgive me.

As a champion racer, I ran with full speed behind him, but he was tough to catch. He was running on the footpath, pushing aside whoever came in his way. Many stalls on the footpath were also pushed and things fell. I continued chasing him, though it was very difficult. Soon he left the footpath and started running on the road. I had a bag on my back, so I was a bit uncomfortable, but I continued nevertheless. I wanted to call the police and inform them, but there was no time for that.

He somehow crossed the road and ran towards the railway station. He must have thought that he would disappear in the crowd on the station. I chased him with all my might. He was on the railway bridge and was running towards the train.

The train halted at the station and I ran towards it. Robert boarded the train compartment and soon, it started. I ran and somehow managed to board the train as well. I saw Robert at the other end of the compartment. The compartment was very crowded so it was difficult to move towards him, but I was trying.

As I reached closer to Robert, he jumped from the running train on the other side of the platform and safely landed there. On an impulse, I also jumped. But, I didn't make it. That was the most painful and regretful moment of my life.

❖

When I tried to jump, my bag got stuck in the gate of the compartment and I didn't reach the ground in the way I wanted to. I got pulled by my bag and fell near the wheels of the train and both of my legs came under it. I screamed. My blood splashed all over my body and face. I felt the pain of my legs getting separated from my body.

When the first two wheels moved, my bones crushed, but my skin was not ready to leave my body. As the next two wheels rolled, they cut my legs. My left leg came completely under the train and my right leg was lost below the knee. I wanted to shout more, but no voice came out of my mouth. I wanted to cry, but my tears became dry.

My legs, my dreams, my life – everything was gone. I was unable to react. Soon the train passed. A huge crowd gathered around me, but no one was ready to pick me up or at least move me aside.

Why did you save me, god? Why didn't you let my whole body come under the train?

I saw the next train coming. I closed my eyes as I didn't want to face people. I wanted to be alone somewhere. I felt like dying. I had ruined Kairav's life and maybe I deserved this because of that. But as I closed my eyes, I saw my parents' faces brimming with love. I was their only hope in life. My father would not want me to do this. I thought about Raj and Kairav; they would be devastated too. The next train came near and I tried to push myself backward. It pained intensely, but I was unable to move by even an inch. The person who loved to run, who had won several competitions in running, was now unable to move. The first tear rolled out of my eyes – the tear of helplessness.

Suddenly a girl, who must be of my age, tried to pull me back.

'Uncle, I am talking to you. Help me to pull the poor guy back,' the girl shouted to a man who was standing close to me. As the girl shouted loudly, many people came closer to me and pulled me back. My white pant had turned red, but had nothing to hold at the ends. The word "poor" said by that girl hurt me a lot. I was now a poor fellow.

I was feeling very guilty as I hadn't taken care of myself. I was irresponsible.

Mustering some courage, I picked the phone and informed my mom. She was inconsolable when she heard about the accident.

More than twenty minutes passed, but no ambulance came to take me to the hospital. Suddenly a coolie came there and picked me up in his arm. A rickshaw stopped and then, the man put me inside it. He removed his red kurta and tied that on my left leg which was bleeding heavily.

It pained a lot in the beginning. But as minutes passed, I was unable to feel my remaining leg. Slowly, my mind stopped working.

The rickshaw took us to the nearest government hospital. I was taken to the ICU immediately. I was waiting for someone to operate on me, but no one came. After a few minutes two policemen entered inside to take my statement. I told them that my legs slipped as the train started as I was standing near the door.

Finally, the doctors came and started dressing the wound. They gave me an injection which put me in a deep sleep.

My eyes were slowly closing, but I knew they were searching for a familiar face. The last song that I had heard came into my mind.

Zindagi ka safar, hai ye kaisa safar...Koi samjha nahi, koi jana nahi...

13

Irreversible

In Raj's voice

45 minutes ago

I left Gorakh at the bus stop and walked towards the station. When I reached college, it was an integrated circuits lecture. In the middle of the lecture, my phone started vibrating. I took it out. it was Gorakh's father. I didn't pick up the call due to the lecture. But then, I received a call from an unknown number. I walked out of the class and took the call.

'Hello,' I said.

'Hello Raj, Mahesh here. There is a serious problem,' the caller replied.

Mahesh was one of our friends in the locality.

'What's the problem bhai?' I asked.

'Gorakh met with a train accident. He is admitted to P.R. Hospital in Kandivali and is very critical. Come soon,' he said.

My legs started shaking and the mobile fell from my hand. I was unable to believe what I had just heard. I rushed inside the class, took my bag, and went outside without asking permission from anyone. P.R. Hospital was half-an-hour away from my college.

I ran as fast as I could towards the hospital. Gorakh's thoughts flooded my mind. A few minutes ago, he was all fine. And now, I didn't know what had happened to my kind-hearted friend. I didn't understand how he reached the railway station when I had left him at the bus stop. I thought of informing Kairav, but I didn't have his mobile number.

I reached the hospital and I asked on the counter there. The lady was doing something on her mobile.

'Ma'am, where is the patient who met with an accident?' I asked.

'Which accident?' the lady asked casually.

'Train accident, please be quick ma'am,' I said.

'When did the accident take place?' she again asked casually.

'Today. Now!' I replied.

'Oh ok, that patient who lost his legs? He is in ICU on the fourth floor,' she said and got busy on her mobile again.

'Lost his legs!' I said. I wanted to shout at the lady at the counter because of her inhumane behaviour.

I ran towards the fourth floor. I reached there, but found no one. I thought I was the first to reach there, but then, I heard a familiar voice.

I walked there and saw Kairav. He was talking to the doctor to start dressing Gorakh's wound. I heard more and came to know that the doctors had not started treating Gorakh as none of his family members or relatives were there. Kairav was forcing the doctor to start the treatment as soon as possible. He also signed a few papers saying he was Gorakh's brother. Thus, the doctor went inside with a few other doctors for dressing up his wounds, but didn't allow Kairav to meet Gorakh.

The doctor went inside and Kairav sat on the chair outside the ICU. He was scratching his head, as if he had gone mad.

When he saw me, he ran towards me. He caught my hand and said, 'Gorakh is our responsibility now. Promise me that we will never leave him alone. Gorakh will always be our priority.'

'I promise Kairav! How is he now?'

With his left hand on his forehead and in a low voice, he said, 'Gorakh lost both his legs, his right leg is gone below the knee and left completely.'

I lost all my energy and senses. Unable to respond, I sat on the nearby chair and held my head.

'There are more problems bhai. 'Gorakh has lost a huge amount of blood and doctors need to do the operation as soon as possible. Mahesh informed me about Gorakh so I immediately came here,' Kairav said.

We were talking further when Gorakh's parents came. We went towards his dad and held him.

'Everything will be fine, uncle. We will handle everything here. Gorakh is our brother,' said Kairav.

The doctor came out after dressing. Kairav and I immediately surrounded him.

'See, we have been able to stop the bleeding, but as I said, the operation is needed urgently so inform me about your decision,' the doctor replied.

'Can we meet him now?' I asked.

'No, the patient is resting,' said the doctor, but then the nurse came out of the ICU and said, 'Sir, the patient woke up, and he is very desperate to meet his parents.'

So the doctor allowed his dad to go inside. Gorakh's mom was crying a lot, so she was not allowed. Taking the opportunity, I went inside the ICU with his father.

'Think before you say anything to him,' said Kairav. I nodded.

Gorakh's dad was very tough. I was unable to read his pain. Gorakh was lying like a small baby on the bed. A very thick dressing was done on both his leg. The left thigh had double the thickness of the right leg dressing. We saw the dressings when the nurse was putting a shawl on his legs. All of a sudden, Gorakh's dad lost his balance, but I held him tight and stopped him from falling. I understood the intense pain he felt after seeing his son's wounds.

Gorakh's eyes were closed.

'Gorakh, wake up beta. It's your dad,' said his father. The sound of Gorakh's dad's voice was so low and painful. I felt his pain in my heart and looked towards his face. I have never seen such a sorrowful face in my life. I don't know how he controlled himself from crying in front of his son, but my eyes went wet. I used my sleeves to wipe the tears and make my eyes look dry.

Gorakh finally opened his eyes. We were very eager to hear his words.

'Thank god you came, papa. I was feeling so lonely,' he said and caught his dad's hand and made him sit closer to himself.

There was a small wound on Gorakh's forehead as well. His dad moved his hand over Gorakh's head and said 'I know you are the strongest. I am always with you.'

'Where is mom?' asked Gorakh.

'She is outside son. Don't worry, she will be coming,' his dad said and went outside, to bring his mother.

Now Gorakh and I were alone. I didn't know what to say. 'Take rest and get well soon. We have a lot to explore.'

When I came out, I told everything to Kairav. We both went to the washroom to wash our faces.

'This is tragic, bhai. I feel like breaking everything here,' said Kairav. I had similar feelings.

'I cannot understand one thing. Gorakh travels by bus, so why did he go at the railway station,' I said.

'Yes, I am thinking the same thing,' he replied.

Suddenly Kairav's mobile rang. After seeing the number, he canceled the call.

Kairav was going to say something to me, but we both were interrupted as Gorakh's dad entered the washroom.

We went towards him and Kairav hugged him. 'Why did this happen to my son when he was at the peak of his life? When he should have been exploring endless possibilities! It is so unfair!

'He gradually took over all my responsibilities. I also started hoping that our life will change in the upcoming years. We were expecting a better future, but now, everything is finished!' He was weeping in front of us. I remembered that day when he shouted at Gorakh in a stern voice when he scored less marks in the HSC exam. Time had changed everyone a lot.

'Uncle, we are always there with him. Don't worry about his future. I am sure it will be brighter than ours,' I said to uncle.

'I know beta. I am counting on both of you but, there is a bigger problem.'

'What's the problem?' asked Kairav.

'The operation which the doctor was talking about will cost 35,000 rupees, and I have nearly 50000 rupees in my account,' uncle replied.

'So what's the problem uncle?' I asked.

'The doctor said that this operation is only the first one. More operations will be required in the coming days. Also, the first operation is the minor one, which means that the other operations will cost even more,' said uncle.

'Don't worry about money, uncle. We will take care of that. You please take care of aunty,' Kairav said.

Oh wow. Is he the same Kairav who ignored us all these years?'

We came out of the washroom and went near the ICU door. Looking inside the ICU through the small glass window made on the door, we saw that Gorakh was sleeping, with drips giving him blood through one hand, and glucose through the other.

He did not deserve it. Deep down, I knew that the repercussions of this tragedy would be irrversible.

14

A Night Below the Stars

In Kairav's voice

It was evening and Gorakh was still sleeping. The nurse gave me the names of the medicines. Raj and I planned to go to the medical shop situated somewhere on the ground floor of the hospital.

Patients were lying on the floor. The hospital was filled with an unbearable smell. Family members of a few patients were trying to find the doctors for hours.

'We have to shift Gorakh from here,' I told Raj.

'What about tomorrow's operation?' he asked.

I was thinking about how we would transfer Gorakh and to which hospital. I didn't answer him. We bought the medicine, went back towards the ICU and gave the medicine to the nurse. I was disconnecting Sapna's call but when I got a moment alone, I called and told her everything.

She wanted to come to see Gorakh, but I stopped her. I didn't want her to see all these things. After talking to her, I came back to Raj.

At night, only one family member was allowed to stay outside the ICU. Hence we decided to sleep somewhere nearby.

'Let's go to the terrace,' I told Raj.

We took two rugs and went to the terrace. Luckily, the door was open. I had already told Gorakh's father that we were going to sleep on the terrace and told him to call whenever needed.

We reached the small concrete room that was made over the terrace for storing water tanks. We decided to sleep over it. Stars were all over the sky.

'How do the patients manage? This carpet is very thin,' said Raj, adjusting himself on the concrete. Ignoring him I said, 'Ask whatever you want to; I know you have various questions.'

'Oh, why not? Let's start from the beginning,' he said.

'Start from wherever you want to, donkey,' I said. I knew he must have felt good to hear donkey from me.

'Did you ever miss us?' he asked. That was quite a silly question.

'Yes, I did miss you both a lot,' I said. I wanted to say more but Raj interrupted me with his next question.

'When you missed us, why didn't you return when Gorakh apologised so many times?'

'If you were in my place, would you have returned? Was saying sorry enough for all that I had to face? Though Gorakh had good intentions, but shouldn't he have asked me before calling the police? Shouldn't he have discussed the plan with both of us first? Keep yourself in my place and then think,' I replied.

He didn't say anything. After nearly five minutes he said, 'Okay, Gorakh made a mistake, but I was nowhere involved in it. Then, why did you say to your dad that you didn't want to see *both* of us?'

'I was in pain, and when we came to know that Gorakh was behind all my sufferings, you immediately took Gorakh's side, so I said that,' I replied.

'Oh my god! What do you expect from a friend when he sees his best friends fighting, I was just trying to resolve your fight. I told you to forgive Gorakh because whatever happened was not in his hand,' he said.

'I know, but I was angry and hurt at that time,' I said.

'Yes, I get it. I wanted to be with you bhai, but you pushed me away,' said Raj. I could understand the pain in his voice. 'You wanted to meet us tonight. Did you forgive us?'

'Yes, I did. I wanted to declare this while eating the Chinese bhel,' I said.

'What took you so long?' he asked tilting towards me.

'I forgave Gorakh a long time back for what happened with me. But his actions had an irretrievable impact on my parents. I bear the consequences of his decision every day. How can I stop thinking about all this? What if Gorakh hadn't called the police that day? Would my mom still be alive?' I told him about the dream where I saw my mom.

'We can never understand your pain bhai, but we will always be with you. I am really sorry for the pain you went through,' he said.

'Forget the past Raj. We have a bigger problem now,' I said.

'What were you saying about shifting Gorakh?' he asked.

'This is a government hospital, so a lot of patients come here. They won't be able to provide proper assistance to Gorakh. So, we will shift Gorakh to Shyamak private hospital,' I replied.

'I think you are correct as this hospital is very far from our locality. Shifting to a nearby hospital will be a good idea bhai, but what about Mehtaji? Did you ask him about this? And though private hospitals will provide better treatment, their cost will be much higher,' said Raj.

'I will handle everything. I have already spoken to the doctor for shifting Gorakh, so it will be done,' I replied.

Raj was looking at me with big eyes. I knew he might be thinking about how I would manage everything. I wanted to tell Raj that after I lost my mother, I just couldn't lose someone else so close to my heart. But, I didn't say that. My friend needed me more than anything else.

Raj was wiping his tears, but I saw him.

'What happened bhai, why are you crying?' I asked him and sat down.

'I also want to help Gorakh. I want to solve all his difficulties, but I am poor and will not be able to do that. When we were young, you and Gorakh shared your tiffin with me. It always consisted of something better than what I had in my tiffin. You guys always helped me, looked after me and never let me feel inferior. At that time, I had decided that someday, I will support you both. I want to help Gorakh in this most difficult phase of his life,' Raj sobbed. I never knew that he felt like this.

'Don't cry bhai, if you would have told me in the beginning, I would have never shared my tasty tiffin with you,' I said and smiled. My joke was successful in making him laugh too.

'In a true friendship, it's not important to repay what your friends do for you. If you are doing something in the hope of getting something in return, then you are not a true friend. You listened to our problems and shared your happiness and sorrows with us. You always did whatever you could to solve our problems. Nothing else is needed.

'I still remember that day, when you fought with Rajat because he hit me. I remember that he hit you so hard that your right eye was swollen for a week. But you fought for me without thinking about the consequences. You are precious. I am blessed to have a friend like you,' I said.

Raj started sobbing more.

'Thank you for defining friendship for me, Kairav.'

❖

My eyes opened at 5:00 a.m. and I woke Raj up as well. We went towards the ICU. Raj's father and mother hadn't slept the whole night and the locality people started coming in the morning itself to see Gorakh. Mrs Mehta was still crying. People were trying to make her eat something. I told Mr Mehta about my plan. Initially, he disagreed, but somehow, Raj and I convinced him.

'All formalities done?' I asked Raj and he nodded. Shyamak hospital's ambulance was waiting outside and we put Gorakh inside it with the oxygen mask. I sat inside the ambulance at the back with Gorakh. Raj sat with the driver.

'Hi, how are you?' said Gorakh in the middle of the journey. It felt like someone had pierced my heart as Gorakh asked about my condition when he was not fine.

'Fine,' I replied with a smile.

'Good to see you bhai,' he said, but it was not good for me to see him in that condition. His mother was caressing his hair. His hand had a glucose needle inside. The oxygen cylinder was on standby for any emergency.

We reached Shyamak hospital. Few ward boys came. They put Gorakh on the stretcher and immediately moved him to the ICU.

The founding member of the Shyamak hospital was my dad's friend, so there was no problem of giving the money immediately. The cost was eighty thousand rupees for the same initial operation, but I had faith in the doctors here.

Within an hour, five doctors assembled and they together visited Gorakh in the ICU.

'All of them have come to visit Gorakh?' asked Mehtaji.

'Yes, uncle,' I replied. I had already told Dr Subhash to consider Gorakh as his son and do everything possible for him. The doctor was a very gentle and kind-hearted person. He called the best surgeon in his contacts. All the doctors had a meeting and then, Dr Subhash called me and Mehta uncle inside.

'We have to do operation today itself in the afternoon, or it will be too late. Gorakh's skin is deteriorating at the wounds and we have to remove the infected skin on priority,' said Dr Subhash.

'Ok doctor, please proceed with the operation, please take care of him,' I said.

We informed everybody about the operation and I went to buy everything required for it.

15

The First Month

In Raj's voice

Gorakh's operation was successful. The unwanted skin was removed. In one month, two more operations were done. It was painful to see Gorakh crying after the operations.

'Why me, mom? What did I do wrong?' he used to say while crying. His mother was also admitted for a few days because of weakness.

Anesthesia stopped working on Gorakh and he turned into an insomniac. Sleeping pills were eaten like chocolates, but had a negligible effect on him. He tried sleeping at night, but was unable to do it. A sudden rise in pain during any time of day occurred regularly. Paracetamol and pain relief tablets were bought in a bunch at the end of the week.

Kairav and I stayed with him all the time. Sometimes, one of us stayed the whole night if an extra bed was available. We used to talk about past moments and jokes to cheer him up.

The third operation was the most painful one, as the doctor cut a small part of Gorakh's left thigh bone so that he could stitch the skin properly. The moment Gorakh came outside, he started crying like a baby. His pain was felt by everyone present there.

Everyone was crying, including his dad. Soon an injection was put in his glucose bottle and he slept.

The cost of the operation and other bills never came to us. Kairav handled everything. He didn't even let me see the bills or tell me about any requirements. Kairav gave his new phone to Gorakh as the hospital had Wi-Fi, so that Gorakh could do whatever he liked. Usually, he stayed awake at nights and watched movies. The best thing about Shyamak hospital was its staff. They behaved like family and took care of everything.

Gorakh still hadn't told us how the accident took place. We didn't even force him to. We were curious to know how he reached the station when he used to go by bus.

❖

My college seminar was postponed by a few days as more students from all over the world were going to attend it, thus more preparation was required. I gave very little time to Robolearn as I took care of Gorakh. The pain of the operation reduced, but the grief of losing both legs never withered away. He often used to feel his legs as if they were there. The feeling of legs though they were not present was called phantom limb condition. Though he used to sleep at night, his legs were always vibrating and shaking.

I was on my way to the railway station from college. Out of nowhere, Kairav jumped in front of me.

'Hi! Surprised, right?' he asked.

'Yes of course, but how are you here bhai? It's your office time,' I said.

'I left early today and was waiting for you here,' he replied.

'Why? Is there any problem?' I asked. All these things that happened somehow made me think that something bad might have happened.

'Shut up Bindiya, and listen. Day after tomorrow is Gorakh's birthday and we will celebrate it. I have already talked with Dr Subhash and he gave me permission for the celebration.'

'How many times I should warn you guys? Never call me Bindiya or consider today to be your last day on earth,' I grunted. 'By the way, brilliant idea bhai!'

We planned to call all our common friends from the locality and school. It was a small surprise party.

We came to Gorakh and saw that he was busy watching something on his mobile. A big smile came on Mrs Mehta's face when she saw us. She used to worry a lot as Gorakh was always busy on his mobile, but whenever we came, we made him talk and move.

'Hi, bhai, what are you watching?' I said.

'Nothing,' replied Gorakh and immediately kept the mobile aside. Something was wrong; we could sense it.

We made Gorakh sit on the wheelchair, and took him towards the balcony. He looked tensed.

'What happened Gorakh, aren't you happy to see me early today?' asked Kairav.

'I saw Robert that day,' he replied.

'Which day? What are you talking about?' asked Kairav impatiently.

Then, Gorakh told us everything that had happened on the day of the accident. Kairav was silent for a few minutes and then went outside. I followed him.

'Where are you going? What happened?' I said and caught his shoulder and turned him towards me.

'That bastard Robert! I will kill him when I find him. That rascal has ruined everything,' he said.

'Calm down bhai! I don't want my friends to be sad. Call the police and inform them about Robert,' I replied. Kairav immediately called the police.

❖

Aunty and I were sitting inside with Gorakh as if nothing special was going to happen. It was Gorakh's birthday. We all wished him and were waiting for our friends to come. Gorakh had no idea about what was going to happen in the next few minutes. After some time, Kairav gave me a missed call and I went outside the ICU.

Nearly thirty-five friends were standing outside. Gorakh was such a nice person that everyone who met him even once became his friend. He was ready to help everyone. I was looking for the planner – the man behind all this. And then, I found someone holding a big box. It was Kairav, with the big cake that he had ordered.

On the count of three, we entered the room and in a few seconds, it was filled with people. Gorakh was extremely surprised to see the crowd and his eyes brightened up.

I selected a broad table and put it near Gorakh's bed. Kairav kept the cake on the table and we both opened it. It was a three-tier chocolate cake. Gorakh cut the cake with a big smile. He was not allowed to eat cake or any outside food, but still, he ate a small piece of it.

It was an amazing moment to see all our friends coming together. It was an auspicious moment, and Gorakh was the celebrity.

After an hour, the ICU was empty again, consisting of the five of us – Gorakh, Kairav, me, and Gorakh's parents. Dr Suhash signaled Kairav to come into his cabin. I also went there with Mehtaji.

'The time has come for the final operation. I consulted an experienced surgeon, and he said that tomorrow, we will be doing the operation and stitching the injuries properly so that prosthetic limbs can be fit in the future,' said Dr Suhash.

This was the first time we realized that prosthetic limbs would be necessary for our friend to walk.

'Prosthetic limbs? Can you tell us more about that?' I asked.

'We will tell you everything about limbs soon after the operation,' replied the doctor.

Mr Mehta became quite worried, but we convinced him that this would be the last operation, and soon Gorakh will walk like before. But the real question was, *will Gorakh walk like before?*

Gorakh was informed about the operation by his mother.

'This is the last operation bhai, and then, we will be back home, having fun like the older days,' Kairav said to Gorakh.

Gorakh was stronger than us. He realized that though we were behaving normally, everyone was worried about the operation.

'Leave all that, give me my gift,' said Gorakh. His question was successful in diverting everyone's mind.

'I have a gift for you man,' said Kairav with a secretive smile.

Everyone was eager to know what Kairav had bought for Gorakh.

'Give it to me then,' said Gorakh. Kairav took out an envelope from his pocket and handed it to Gorakh. The envelope consisted of a letter. Gorakh read the entire printed letter and then, handed it over to his father. He didn't look happy.

'This letter says that the ITT training exam result is out. Gorakh has passed the exam, keeping his previous performance in mind, even though he didn't give the exam due to his accident,' said Mehtaji.

Kairav gave an application letter to the CA institution after the ITT exam telling the officials about Gorakh's condition. He also submitted the presentation project that Gorakh was supposed to submit. Thus the officials passed Gorakh. Now, Gorakh had to do the internship for three years. After passing the IPCC exam, he would be a CA. I realized that sometimes, the most precious gifts does not require even a single penny.

'Wonderful job bhai, it's a precious gift,' I said.

'Yes it's good news,' said Gorakh with a fake smile.

We realized that Gorakh was now least interested in doing CA.

❖

The next morning, we reached the hospital and soon, the operation started. It took three hours and soon the surgeon with Dr Suhash came out of the OT.

'The operation was successful. Now, we have to wait for his wounds to heal. After a few days, we will start his exercises for walking, and soon he will start walking with a prosthesis. There is nothing to worry about. We just added some stitches and removed a few of the previous ones. Now, there is no need for further operations,' said the surgeon.

Gorakh was brought out on the stretcher, and then, we put him on his bed. The pain was increasing slowly as the effect of anesthesia was reducing. The doctor refused to give the sleep-inducing injection thinking that Gorakh's body will get used to it. Gorakh was asking for it, so the doctor took water in the injection and put it in the glucose bottle. Gorakh saw that and soon, he fell asleep.

My mobile vibrated a few minutes after Gorakh had slept. It was a call from Gaurav, the Robolearn committee's head.

'Tomorrow is the seminar and you didn't come to the college today! Where are you?' Gaurav asked.

'I am in the hospital because today was Gorakh's operation,' I replied.

'Oh, I hope everything is fine. Actually I urgently need you for the seminar, man. We have decided that you will host the seminar,' said Gaurav.

'Me? Host? Never,' I replied.

'Yes, you have to host because Bhola is not feeling well. I will be busy arranging everything, so the next person is you,' he replied. 'We really need you this time.'

'I will be there tomorrow,' I said and hung up.

16

She Looked Back

On the seminar day, when I reached the college, I was surprised to see nearly twenty police mobile vans and many commandos surrounding the college. The big college entrance was now reduced to a narrow gate by wooden rods so that only one person could enter at a time. I went near the narrow passage.

'Who are you? Where is your entrance pass?' asked a commando standing there with a big gun in his hand.

'I am a student of the college,' I said.

'Which college?' he asked.

'This college,' I said. I realized that I hadn't worn the college ID card. I was allowed inside after showing it. Gaurav was waiting for me inside. He took me inside a classroom. I saw a few police officers inside as well.

'Why is the police here?' I asked.

'This is what happens when you do not attend the preparation discussions,' he said. He looked quite tensed.

'Please understand that this seminar is not like ordinary seminars that we have handled before. Dr Govind Lal Batta is an influential man. This security is for him. Students from all over the world are coming to attend the seminar. And what is this? You came in a t-shirt on such an important day. I knew you would do something like this, that's why I brought this formal suit for you,' said Gaurav.

I took the suit and tried to ease his stress. 'See, here is the schedule. Accordingly prepare yourself, and here is your pass so that you can be present around the stage. All the best bhai.'

As Gaurav moved from there, I called Kairav. He informed me that he was leaving for the house from the hospital, and would later go to the office from there.

After wearing the coat, I decided to have a look at the schedule. I came to know that I had to first welcome the students with a few other members of the committee. They were going to arrive early.

And then, after the security check, Mr Batta would come with his colleagues and demonstrate the working of the robot which he had designed. I went towards the entrance with the Bluetooth device in my ear. I called Mohan, Raghav and other members to come to the entrance for welcoming students and other guests.

One by one, the students started entering inside. I had a handshake with everyone and greeted them and Mohan was guiding them towards the auditorium. Seats were already booked for people, and the number of people entering the college were also fixed. Suddenly reporters from various news channels and newspapers started pouring in.

'Why is media here, Gaurav?' I asked.

'For the coverage, obviously,' he replied.

I was already nervous about hosting the seminar, and now after seeing the media, I became more anxious.

People were still entering, and I was already getting exhausted. Standing out in the hot weather was an added headache. I had no idea that my life was going to change in some moments.

'Madam, please remove the dupatta from your face as we need to match your face with the picture on your ID,' said the commando, standing at the main entrance.

The hot weather had forced the girl to cover her head and face. She was wearing a light pink salwar kameez which complemented her pink purse and earrings. I was looking at her while greeting the others. She gradually removed the dupatta from her face. I was stunned. She was beautiful. She had big blue eyes and her long shiny braided hair reached her waist. Her pale skin looked golden from where I was standing. I fell in love with her the moment I saw her.

'Beautiful,' I said. Everyone connected to the Bluetooth heard it.

'You idiot! Stop staring at her, and come back to your senses,' said Mohan.

I realized that I had stopped shaking hands and greeting people. I controlled myself and tried to turn my face towards others. I was waiting for her turn and then, she arrived.

'Good morning, I…We…' I said, while shaking my hand with her.

My heart beat rapidly, and my tongue stopped working. I wanted to say something, but no words came out of my mouth. For the first time, I felt that I could just be with someone for my entire life. It was an unbelievable moment for me.

When she shook hands with me, I touched her soft hands. I felt like the lines on my palm fit in perfectly with hers, and the pattern matched, like a security pattern.

'Good morning,' she replied in her melodious voice. 'We?'

'Sorry…Sorry, I meant we are grateful to have you here,' I said.

'Oh, thank you, shall I go inside?' she asked, looking towards me strangely, as her hand was still in mine.

'Yes, please,' I replied, leaving her hand. Mohan guided her towards the auditorium.

My heart was beating in her direction. I knew it was love and that we were made for each other.

'What happened bhai? You look as if you lost something,' asked Mohan.

'Yes, I lost my heart,' I replied.

'Looks like someone is in love,' he said and patted my back. 'Now let's concentrate on the seminar, all guests are inside.'

We went inside on the first floor in the auditorium. My eyes started scanning the students at the back to find the girl. I saw all the chairs but was unable to find her. I was desperate to see her again.

'There is Gaurav,' said Mohan and we went towards him.

'Thank god you are here. Mr Batta is on time and will be reaching here in fifteen minutes,' said Gaurav and handed me some printed pages.

'What's this?' I asked.

'These are Mr Batta's achievements. As soon as Mr Batta arrives, you have to introduce him to everyone here. Please, do it nicely,' he requested.

'Don't worry, I will handle it efficiently,' I assured him though I was not so sure myself.

I started reading about Mr Batta and realized that he was a true legend.

Soon the world-famous scientist arrived, and our principal went to receive him at the entrance. He entered the auditorium.

He was wearing a white shirt and black pants. Surrounded by many people and two bodyguards, Mr Batta sat on the special chair on the stage.

Our principal and director were also sitting along with him and his colleagues. I took the name of Lord Hanuman in my mind and asked for his help. I was standing at the right side of the stage and others were sitting in the middle. I adjusted the microphone and started.

'Good morning to everyone present here. My name is Raj Ojha. As we all know, today is not an ordinary day for us, because we are sharing this auditorium with an extraordinary person. We are delighted to have students, professors, and other dignitaries present here from all over the world. We are here to listen to Mr Govind Lal Batta, who has so many achievements that it will be difficult to tell each of them. I would try my best to tell you everything about him, though. Let's start from the beginning.'

It was going so perfectly until I saw my girl behind. She was sitting at the back. The moment I saw her, I paused. I felt as if there is nothing between her and me.

'Raj, you idiot, say something, you are on the stage, quick,' someone said on the Bluetooth.

I got back to my senses and started speaking again, but my eyes were still stuck to the chair. Everyone was looking eagerly at me.

I said, 'Sometimes when we see something, we are drawn towards it so much that a feeling enrages within our heart. We are ready to do anything to achieve it, even if it requires us to overcome any adversity. Nothing else except our passion remains, everything else become unimportant.' The moment I said this, the whole auditorium started murmuring.

'What are you saying Raj? We are not here to talk about love,' said Mohan.

'He will ruin everything. Oh my god, why did I hand him the mike,' said Gaurav in anger. I realized that I had gotten carried away by my feelings. Something had to be done. I saw people making strange faces. I saw her smiling at the back and I saw the camera that was focused on me.

'This is how Mr Batta is passionate about robotics. When he was young, he fell in love with robots. He worked hard to create one of the most advanced robots "K271PUPA" ever made by an Indian. Give a huge round of applause everyone, for Batta sir.'

There was a moment of silence. I was getting demotivated, but someone from the back started to clap. Then, the whole auditorium started clapping.

Soon I finished my speech, and then called Mr Batta to share his views.

'Good morning everyone,' he said cheerfully, and the whole auditorium responded. I could see from the corner of the stage how eager everyone was to listen to him.

'This is not the first time I have been to any college or any seminar, but I am overwhelmed today by listening to how that guy, what's your name son?' he asked.

I was shocked that he asked me my name.

'Raj sir, Raj,' I replied.

'Oh yes, Raj Ojha, by listening to how Raj introduced me. Whenever anyone usually introduces me, they speak so mechanically that sometimes I feel I am a machine,' he said.

Everyone laughed.

'No, it's true. The real thing that no one understands is passion, as truly said by Raj. I am passionate about robotics; it took almost two years for us to build K271PUPA. It is a result of extreme hard work and dedication,' he explained.

Mr Batta went on speaking about PUPA – how it functions and who was involved in the project, but I was thinking just about my girl. I was looking towards her and suddenly, she looked at me too. I started looking at Mr Batta.

Mr Batta finished his part of the seminar, and then, others came and presented their speeches.

The seminar was over and for lunch, everyone went to the ground floor hall.

I was waiting for her to pass as I was again standing near the exit door of the auditorium. All of a sudden, Gaurav grabbed my hand and pulled me back.

'Control bhai, don't make your feelings so evident by staring,' he said.

'Oh really?' I asked.

'Yes, why not? You should stare in a way that no one realizes what you are actually up to. But you seem to lose control.' He smiled.

'I like her,' I said slowly, and then she moved towards the exit door. She was with a few more girls, but I looked only at her.

'Oh my god, she is so beautiful, isn't she?' I said.

'Yes, she is,' replied Mohan.

I gave an angry look to him.

'My beautiful bhabi,' chuckled Mohan. I patted his shoulders. 'Do you want her name and her college name?' He removed the Bluetooth from his ear.

'You are my best friend, I knew that the moment I saw you,' I said and hugged him.

'Stop the drama, lover boy! Listen, we have to ask Poonam to show us the list of the students who came today. She was ticking beside their names while they entered the college,' said Mohan.

'Nice plan bro, we will show the girl to Poonam, and when she will sign while leaving, Poonam will remember her details and tell us,' I said impatiently.

'Yes, but Gaurav should not know about this,' he replied. I agreed.

Lunch was over and gradually everyone was leaving the college. Mr Batta was the first to leave due to security issues. I was standing near the gate. I was already feeling sad that she was leaving. It's strange how someone can become so important in such a short time.

I saw her moving towards the single exit door. I felt like stopping her and telling her that I was in love with her. It was a surge of feelings that I had never experienced before.

She signed the sheet and went out of the small gate. I wanted to go after her.

'Simran,' whispered Mohan in my ears.

'What?' I asked.

'Her name is Simran, Raj,' he said with a very big smile on his face.

I remembered the movie DDLJ. In the movie, Shahrukh's name was Raj and Kajol's name was Simran. I felt as if god had signalled me to calm down and have faith in him. I remembered the scene when the hero says that if the girl looks back at you, then she also loves you.

I ran outside the gate. I tried to find her. I saw that she was taking a rickshaw and she sat inside it. The rickshaw started moving. I was looking towards the rickshaw and then, magic happened. I don't know why but she looked outside the rickshaw towards the gate. That was the most beautiful face I ever saw.

In a moment, we looked at each other. She smiled, I blushed. And then, her beautiful long hair also came out.

I sat on the ground on my knees. I felt as if I had got everything in that moment. Then the rickshaw with Simran went so far that I couldn't see anything. Mohan also came outside he turned my face towards him.

'I wasn't done telling everything and you ran away, don't you want to know her college?' said Mohan.

'Yes, I want to know, tell me,' I replied and stood up, holding my chest.

'She is from our own college, but the Patoha branch,' he answered.

I was happy that she belonged to our college, but would have been much happier if it was our branch.

It was the most beautiful day of my life.

17

Let's Walk

In Gorakh's words

'You love that girl, I can't believe it!' I said.

'I love her,' said Raj. His expressions showed that he had genuine feelings for that girl.

'Now, since we are talking about girls, Kairav can you tell us something about the girl whose call you disconnect whenever we are nearby,' said Raj.

As Raj said this, Kairav's mobile rang and Raj snatched it from his hand.

'Oh, Sapna, now I know who she is,' said Raj and took her call.

'Nothing like that,' said Kairav and snatched back the mobile.

'If there is nothing like that, then why don't you talk to her in front of us?' murmured Raj with his usual smile.

'Ok, why not!' said Kairav and picked up the call.

'Hello Sapna! What happened?'

'Yes, you can do it.'

'I am in the hospital right now.'

'Ok, I will do it,' said Kairav and cut the call.

'Now it's okay, right? Now you both believe me that there is nothing between us. We both work together, that's it!' said Kairav acting casual.

'Give me your mobile for a second,' said Raj.

Kairav gave the mobile, looking towards him in anger.

'I switched on the call recorder after picking up the call, and now let's hear the real conversation,' said Raj. Kairav's face turned red. He again tried to take the mobile, but was unsuccessful. And the conversation started...

Kairav: Hello Sapna! What happened?

Sapna: What do you mean by what happened. I was missing you, so I called you my koochipoochi. Can't I call you without any reason?

Kairav: Yes, you can do it.

Sapna: I love you, my baby.

Kairav: I am in the hospital right now.

Sapna: Oh sorry, I disturbed you, baby. See you soon my teddy. Take care.

Kairav: Ok, I will do it.

Kairav's blush told us everything.

'There's nothing like it; she is just a friend,' said Kairav shying.

'Yeah, we both got it, baby,' I said, and after so many days, I laughed.

Dr Subhash told us that after a week, a trainer would come and train me for walking with the prosthesis. He would tell the exercises that I have to do for it, and then soon, I would be discharged.

❖

The trainer was a girl. She was very punctual and strict. She made me do various exercises and soon, the discharge date arrived.

I was in the hospital for more than three months and went through various treatments. It was a private hospital and the bed cost for one day was four thousand rupees. I was thinking about the expenses all the time. I decided to ask dad about the hospital bills.

'We will be leaving from here in two hours,' said Raj.

'Where is Kairav?' I asked.

'He is at your home, ensuring that everything there is perfect,' said Raj.

I was feeling proud and lucky to have friends like them. They took care of everything very well. I didn't have to ask for anything. Many relatives came in the initial months to see me, but then, their visits reduced. My eyes filled with tears when I thought about their intense care and love that my friends had showered upon me.

My dad arrived and sat close to me, caressing my head. He kissed my forehead and said, 'Beta, you are the strongest person I know.' But I had something else going on in my mind.

'Dad, how much is the hospital bill?'

He looked a bit tensed and said, 'Beta, first you reach home, and then I will answer all your questions.' I didn't force him and decided to wait for that moment.

'Sign here,' said Dr Subhash and I signed on the discharge form. I sat in the wheelchair, and Raj went down to look for the taxi. My mom gave twenty rupees each to the caretakers who had treated me as their son. They wished me luck for the future.

'I got the taxi, let's go,' said Raj. I was sitting in the wheelchair and my father pushed it towards the gate, and then, both of them made me sit inside the taxi.

After so many days, I was sitting inside a vehicle and would also face the outside world. I was supposed to be discharged in the morning, but I insisted on afternoon, so that fewer people would be present on the ground. I felt embarrassed. It was difficult to see old faces at the old place, who would now see me differently.

The taxi was moving and my heart was beating faster. Finally, I reached the ground and took my head out of the taxi window to see if there were people on the ground.

There was a small crowd, as always. I saw Kairav waiting for us. The taxi stopped, and the wheelchair kept upon the taxi was brought down by Raj. My dad and Raj took me out and made me sit in the wheelchair. Soon, people started coming. I could hear their murmur. As the passage towards my chawl had ups and downs and many holes, they had to lift the wheelchair a number of times.

As we moved forward, more and more people came behind us. Soon, I saw my house and felt relieved. They took me inside. In a minute, my house was filled with many people of our society. They were discussing among themselves about me and my accident. I was feeling very uncomfortable.

As if Raj and Gorakh understood my feelings.

'We have to change his dress, so please can you all give some privacy?' Raj said.

Many aunties looked towards Raj in disbelief and then, they moved out.

As they left the house, Kairav locked the door from inside, and then we all heaved a great sigh of relief. I tried to move on the bed from the wheelchair on my own. I exerted some force on the bed and picked myself up, to place myself on the bed. I tried hard, but was unable to do that.

I felt sad, but then, Kairav kept his hand on my shoulder and said, 'See, this is your first target, first try moving on the bed, and then with practice, you will start doing everything like before.'

By seeing his belief, I too felt motivated, but I knew that there was a huge difference between saying that "the thing will happen", and the "thing actually happening".

❖

It was 11 at night.

'Ok guys, my mom is calling, I have to go, but remember, I am a call away,' said Raj.

'Yeah, see you in the morning,' replied Kairav.

'Kairav, you will stay here today?' I asked him.

'His wish! This house belongs to him as well,' my mom said, looking towards me in anger.

'Bhai, I decided to stay with you for a few days,' said Kairav.

I was happy that he will stay with me, but something fishy was going on, and I understood it.

Kairav slept at the side of my bed below on the floor, on a mattress. I turned a bit to see his face. He was looking calm, but mosquitos irritated him. Though a mosquito repellant vaporizer was on, it barely had any effect. Kairav was moving uncomfortably and I realized that the hard floor made him feel uncomfortable as the mattress was thin. I knew that the next day, he would buy a thick mattress or maybe another bed. But the thought that Kairav had to see these difficult days because of me made me unhappy. Lost in thoughts, I drifted to sleep.

Kairav and Raj were present when I woke up. It was Sunday and they had planned to take me out, but I had something else going in my mind.

'Dad, how much was the hospital bill and how did you arrange the money?' I asked. There was pin-drop silence for a moment, and everyone looked towards each other.

'Now you are out of the hospital bhai, no further treatments. So forget about that and get ready, we have to go out,' said Kairav.

'I will not go anywhere until you all tell me everything in detail,' I said, folding my hands in anger.

'He should know everything,' said Raj and I saw Kairav hitting him with his elbow.

'Kairav beta, let Raj speak,' said dad.

'Admitted for more than three months in a private hospital, it is understandable that the bills must be high,' said Raj.

'How much was the bill?' I asked.

'It cost nearly eleven lakh and forty-five thousand rupees,' replied Raj.

'When uncle heard the amount, he panicked as he was able to arrange only one lakh rupees. The initial treatment costs and other things required money as well, so he decided to sell the house,' added Raj.

'Oh, it means we have sold this house,' I said with wet eyes.

'No Gorakh. Uncle thought of selling the house, but Kairav stopped him. He decided to pay the bill.'

'How did Kairav arrange such a high amount?' I asked.

'I sold the house I had bought. It was always dirty and there were lots of rats in that house. Also, I was getting thin by eating outside food, so I decided to stay in a house where I would get a tasty meal and no rats. I had to sell the house, and I got twelve lakh rupees. Coincidentally uncle needed the money so I just helped him. Your kind parents allowed me to live here till I find a new place,' said Kairav.

'What have you done Kairav? You sold your new house for me!' I said. My heart was aching.

'No, no brother, I sold it before uncle needed money. As I said, it's just a coincidence,' said Kairav.

He acted as if I was a fool to not understand that he sold the house for paying my bills. He knew that if my dad would sell his house, we would have nowhere to go. I didn't know what to say. I didn't know how to thank him for his unflinching loyalty.

'We will go to the park,' said Raj.

They made me sit in a wheelchair. We were on the ground.

'How's our stadium looking?' asked Raj.

'As it used to,' I replied.

'What happened brother? Do you want to say something?' said Kairav.

'Why did you sell your house? There must have been some other way to pay the bill. Why do you always want to be the bigger person? Who does so much for a friend who is of no use now?' I burst into tears.

'First stop crying Gorakh, and then I will speak,' said Kairav. I wiped my tears.

'What do you mean by *a friend who is of no use*? Friendship isn't transactional. Your problems are ours. We are not doing it for you, we are doing it for ourselves. Also, I honestly didn't like that house; it was too lonely there and I was going to sell it soon. I wanted to stay with you all. Aren't you happy with me living in your house?' he said.

'I am happy,' I replied, wiping my nose.

'The topic ends here then. Also if I wished, I could have shifted to Sapna's house, but I wanted to stay here in the locality where my friends live,' said Kairav.

'Oh, living with Sapna or live-in with Sapna?' asked Raj.

'Here we go again,' said Kairav.

'Kick me, my teddy,' said Raj. We all laughed as we had when we were returning from Marine Drive not long ago.

❖

We were in the park and then, I had to return as the trainer was going to come that day. Her name was Mitali.

The daily exercise was finished, and then, she said, 'Now you are ready Gorakh.'

'Ready for what?' I asked.

'Ready for walking,' she said smiling.

'Now you can think about buying the prosthesis for him, but first take the free prosthesis from Bhagwan Mahavir Vikalang Sahayata Samiti, and practice with it,' she said.

She told us the entire process. In the Samiti, free prosthetic legs were given to people like me. Initially, we had to go there once so that they could take the measurements and make the prosthesis of my size. And then, they would call when it was ready.

We decided to go the next day.

Kairav, mom, Raj and I all went together to the Samiti. We were shocked to see many differently-abled people present there. Few were walking with the help of the prosthesis, while others were in the queue for giving their measurement.

We also sat in the queue and in two hours, the procedure was completed. They told us to come back in fifteen days for the prosthesis.

In these fifteen days, the trainer made me do lots of exercises so that I was physically ready for walking. My disability certificate was also made. I was 92% disabled as per the certificate issued to me. The day finally arrived for which my family members and my friends were more eager than I was. They finally brought the prosthesis.

The prosthetic legs were very hard, so I had to wear long socks on my legs before putting those.

'Wouldn't it hurt him? It's hard plastic,' said Kairav to Mitali.

'It will, in the beginning, but afterward, it won't,' she replied.

'Try to stand up now,' said Mitali in her usual stern tone when I was ready. I tried to, but I was unable to do that. I lifted myself a bit upward, but soon, fell on the bed again. The trainer was standing in front of me. Kairav helped me stand up.

My hand was on his shoulder and I was finally standing on my legs. They were *my* legs now.

My daily task included standing wearing those prostheses for as much time as I could. The second step was to try to move slowly. As my right leg had a knee, I was able to move it a bit ahead of me. But, it was very difficult to do the same with the left leg.

After practising for two weeks, I was able to move both my legs, but still, the left leg was a problem. I had to first lift the left leg with the help of my waist and then, keep it in front. Kairav brought two sticks for me so that I could walk using the stick instead of holding hands.

I used to take one stick in my right hand and then catch someone's hand with my left hand to move slowly around the house.

'Today we will go out and you will walk outside,' declared Kairav. It was a Sunday. Mitali stopped coming to train me as we were not able to afford her. I had already learned the basics of walking with prosthesis.

Raj caught my hand and I walked out of my locality in the stadium. I walked slowly and so did they. We reached a bit away from our locality.

'Now try walking without holding Raj's hand,' said Kairav.

'Are you mad?' I said as I thought he was joking. I looked towards him to see his face, but they both were serious.

'How can I? I am sure I will fall in the next step,' I said.

'We will not let you fall,' said Kairav.

I was motivated to give it a try.

'If I fall, I will break your heads with my stick,' I said. Kairav stood in front and Raj behind me. Raj left my hand and I stood still in the middle of them.

It was a decisive moment for me.

'Try bhai,' said Kairav.

I lifted my right leg and kept it a few inches ahead, and lost balance, but the stick kept me upright. Then, I kept my stick in the front and finally put my left leg ahead. It was my first step after months. I was happy, but the people who forced me to do that were happier. I could see the joy on their faces.

I took a few more steps. And finally, the impossible came true. I walked.

18

The Three Problems

In Raj's voice

We had a dinner party to celebrate Gorakh's walk. Gorakh walked to the hotel without holding our hand, but he got too tired and sweaty. We were thinking about buying a new prosthetic leg for him, which would be more comfortable and easier to walk with.

After the party, I returned home. I wanted to stay longer with Gorakh, but had to write lots of assignments and tutorials. But then, Kairav called me and asked to meet on the ground. I changed the dress and reached there.

'Hi Raj,' he said.

'Hi, what happened? Why did you call me? Any problem?' I asked.

'I wanted to discuss something important,' he said.

'Yes, tell me.'

'I have no money left.' He looked very sad.

'Let's loot a bank then,' I said with a smile, trying to lighten his mood.

'Let it be bhai, there is no point of telling you anything. You leave it on me and please go,' he said and started walking away.

'Why will I leave it on you, I care about Gorakh too,' I shouted, losing my temper.

'Ask yourself, what you have done for him that no one else could do?'

'I always did whatever was possible for me. You have a job, you earn, I don't. So how I can buy things?'

'Very good bhai, you are more idiotic than I thought. I am talking about what have you done for him, and you are hiding your careless attitude behind money,' he said.

'Careless?' I didn't understand what Kairav was trying to say.

'Yes, you are careless. You only look in the present. Everything is a joke for you.'

'Shut up Kairav,' I shouted, catching the collar of his shirt. 'Who the hell do you think you are? I know you did a lot for Gorakh, but that doesn't make me your slave. You can't ask me to change my habits just because you don't like them.'

'Get lost.'

'What?'

'Get lost from our life,' Kairav said.

I left his collar and went home with tears in my eyes. I didn't know what happened to Kairav all of a sudden. I was unable to sleep that night.

❖

The next morning, I went to Gorakh's house. I was trying to find Kairav as he used to leave for office with me from there.

'Where is Kairav?' I asked Gorakh.

'He went to the office. He left early in the morning today as he had lots of work to do,' replied Gorakh. I knew that Kairav was angry with me, so he left early.

I reached college and the lecture started. The lecture was quite interesting as the subject was Digital Communication, but my fight with Kairav didn't let me concentrate.

The next lecture was going to start, but then the peon arrived with some notice and took permission from the lecturer to announce it.

From next week, students of J.K. Institute, Patoha branch will come here in our college for their lectures as the Patoha branch building is under renovation. Students of our college are ordered to maintain proper discipline. The students of the Patoha branch will be taught here. This will be their college as well until their college renovation gets completed.

A wave of happiness ran through me. All my anger disappeared in a moment. I was blushing. The thought of Simran sitting besides me was so exhilarating.

After reaching home, I decided to tell Gorakh about this wonderful news. It was 5:00 p.m. As I reached, I found Gorakh having tea. I immediately went inside and hugged him. I told him about the good news.

'Oh my god, you are so lucky bhai! I am very happy for you,' he said with his pleasant smile.

'Did you tell Kairav about this? He will also be very happy and shocked,' he said.

'I didn't tell Kairav anything, he is very rude. I don't know what he thinks of himself,' I answered, ignoring Kairav's topic.

'Why are you saying this? Tell me what's the matter?' asked Gorakh.

'Nothing much, he was telling me that I don't think of the future, I am very careless and useless as well.'

'He must have joked,' said Gorakh.

'He was not joking; he said all these things in anger. If he would have been joking, then I wouldn't have felt so bad,' I said.

'He never says such things. Then he might be very tensed,' said Gorakh.

'Let there be any reason, but he cannot talk to me like this,' I said and sat on the bed with him.

'It's not like that. You take your time to understand. I will not force you,' he said.

'Yes, let's see,' I replied.

I was in his house and he was practising his walk.

'This hurts a bit,' said Gorakh, sitting on the bed and adjusting his prosthetic legs. It was difficult to walk with the prosthesis. The left knee was not automatically bendable. Gorakh had to first sit and then, push a bolt so that the leg could be bent on the knee. And then, when he wanted to make it straight again, at the time of walking, he had to pull back the bolt to its initial position.

'In a few days, you will get used to it. Then, it will not hurt bhai. It is like wearing a new chappal,' I said.

'Waiting for that day,' he replied.

And then, Kairav arrived. He had a plastic bag in his hand. He always used to bring something to eat whenever he returned home. He saw me, but didn't react much.

'Hi bhai, I was waiting for you,' said Gorakh with a pleasant smile. He used to become very happy on seeing Kairav.

'What happened? Is it hurting again?' he asked Gorakh.

'Yes, a bit,' said Gorakh.

'Don't worry bhai, soon we will do something about it. I am thinking about buying a new comfortable and better prosthesis,' said Kairav.

'Oh really, a better prosthesis? But that would be expensive, right?' said Gorakh.

Kairav didn't react to that and said, 'Gorakh, will it be okay if I stay at Sapna's house tonight?' He tried to act serious, but Gorakh started fake coughing.

'It's okay my boy, we understand your feelings. Isn't it Raj?' said Gorakh.

'Yes,' I replied.

'It's the day I proposed to her,' said Kairav, blushing a bit.

'Control teddy, control,' said Gorakh. He left after some time for Sapna's house. The whole time, he didn't even try to talk to me; nor did I.

'We forgot to tell him about Simran,' said Gorakh. He started the exercise again.

'That's fine. Kairav also wanted to do engineering, right?' I said.

'Yes, but sadly he didn't get the opportunity. All my fault,' wailed Gorakh.

'No, it's not,' I said, gently patting his back. 'I guess Kairav is jealous of me.'

'What?' asked Gorakh. He came near me and stood catching my shoulder.

'I am studying engineering, though the chances were very less, and he was unable to do. It. I think he is jealous of me, and that's why he misbehaved,' I said, looking towards Gorakh to check his views.

'Have you lost it? You are such a fool,' said Gorakh to me. 'You are going off track.'

'You didn't see what I saw,' I said.

'And you don't know what I know,' he said.

'What are you talking about? What do I not know about? Tell me,' I said.

'Nothing bhai, I am saying that you are getting it wrong. Kairav always thinks good about everybody,' said Gorakh.

'Don't try to hide anything from me. Tell me what I don't know,' I said. 'I knew that you were hiding something from me. That's why I said that Kairav is jealous, so that you would tell me the truth.'

'Okay, I will tell you. Kairav intentionally told you all those things yesterday. He wanted you to get angry so that you leave us,' he said sitting on the bed. I was shocked to hear it.

'Why bhai? Why? What were you guys planning? Did I do something wrong? Why do both of you don't want me in your life?' I shouted. 'Gorakh…Gorakh, you can't keep your mouth shut?' said Kairav entering the house.

'Hush, thank god you are here Kairav, I can't do it bhai,' said Gorakh. 'Weren't you going to Sapna's place?'

'She had to go somewhere urgently, so we cancelled the plan,' said Kairav sitting beside Gorakh.

'Will someone tell me what is going on?' I asked impatiently.

'You should leave us, Raj. You can't be with us,' said Kairav.

'Why?' I shouted.

'For yourself bhai, so that nothing wrong happens with you as well,' Kairav shouted back.

'I didn't get you,' I said. I sat at the table nearby.

'Do you remember the panditji we met outside the Siddhivinayak temple? Do you remember what he said?' asked Gorakh. I recollected everything and soon, I realized what they were trying to do.

'The pandit warned us to stay away from each other, but we didn't listen. Now see what happened with me and Gorakh. I lost my mom and Gorakh lost his legs. We don't want anything to happen to you bhai, please understand,' said Kairav.

I had no words, just tears in my eyes. Kairav came towards me to comfort me, but I pushed him away. I was angry.

'So you both thought that you will trick me into leaving you? Do you think I will ever leave you both? And Kairav, you said yourself that whatever that pandit said was stupid, then why are you doing all this? And, even if the pandit was right, I don't give a damn. I am never leaving you alone,' I said and cried.

'We will together face anything that comes our way,' I said. Gorakh walked towards us and we hugged.

'There is one more thing we hid from you, Raj. It's about your admissions,' said Gorakh.

'Let's eat the mangoes I bought. Now Raj isn't leaving us, so we will have to share,' said Kairav.

'Bhai, he should know what you did,' said Gorakh to Kairav

'Kairav was the person behind your admissions.'

'What?' I said in surprise.

'Yes. The officer didn't realize his mistake. Kairav paid the clerk of the Dangoba House office to call you and get your income certificate made in a day. Luckily Kairav had met Nitin and he told him about the income certificate issue,' he said.

We were all quiet for some time.

'Mangoes anyone?' said Kairav trying to change the subject.

'I will have one,' I said and walked towards the kitchen to bring the knife.

❖

'After eating the mangoes, I went out for a walk with Kairav. We reached the stadium and sat on the chairs there.

'I am not going to thank you,' I said. Kairav looked towards me strangely. 'I am not going to disrespect what you did for me and Gorakh by a mere 'thank you'. Whatever you said in the morning about me is true. I am careless.'

'That's not true. I said all those things to make you angry, that's it.'

'I know bhai, but I know I am irresponsible. But not anymore. I have realized many things today, and it's time for me to grow up and be responsible.'

'If that's what you think, so be it. I only want your betterment,' said Kairav and got lost in his thoughts.

'You looked tensed bhai, tell me what's wrong,' I asked.

'I have no money left. Why does everything stop at money? How many more days will Gorakh be at home? He is not so comfortable with the prosthesis as well. I would have bought the better prosthesis, but I have no money,' said Kairav. I wished I could help in some way.

'We have to think of something, I can't even get a loan as I sold my house. The prosthesis cost is around 4 lakhs. Gorakh's dad said that he can arrange 80,000 rupees, and we got 40, 000 rupees from the trust, but the remaining 2,80,000 rupees… where will we get that from?' said Kairav.

'We will do something bhai. Let me also think about it,' I said. Kairav patted my back.

'We also have to think about Gorakh's studies,' I said.

'Yes, now he has to give the IPCC exams to become a CA.'

'But before that, he will have to do a nine-month articleship under a CA.'

'That's the real problem bhai! How will Gorakh be able to do the field work? Office work can be done once he reaches the office, but the main problem is field work. We will also have to find a CA who will keep Gorakh as an employee for the articleship.'

'I think the biggest problem is to convince Gorakh to start studying for CA again.'

19

The Happy Donot

In Raj's voice

We had decided to talk to Gorakh about our plan to make him study further. We were in his house watching TV. It was late afternoon. Uncle and aunty had gone to the temple.

'I would like to ask you both something,' said Kairav.

I switched off the TV as I knew what was going on.

'Tell me, what's the one thing that remains with a person even after everything is lost? I mean, if a man loses all his money, what can never be taken from him?'

'His knowledge,' said Gorakh.

'Awesome, it's the right answer,' said Kairav. 'But my actual question is, where does knowledge come from? What is human life without knowledge?'

'Knowledge comes from studying and with experiences. And, human life without knowledge is aimless, I guess,' said Gorakh.

'Exactly, you are so smart,' said Kairav.

'Talking about studying, Gorakh, when are you going to start studying again?' I asked as we had planned before.

'What will I study now? I forgot everything that I used to know. I am thinking of doing a business or something.'

'What will you study now? You were preparing for IPCC. Continue that,' said Kairav.

'I can't bhai, it's very difficult for me now. When I was fine, I was going to do it with the help of classes, and still wasn't sure that I would pass or not. But now, it's not my cup of tea,' said Gorakh.

'If you will never try, then how will you come to know whether you can do it or not?' I said.

'Do you both think I didn't try? I tried to study, I opened the book, but everything is blank in my mind. I can't do CA now,' said Gorakh.

'You can do it. With a little practice, you will be back on track. You will succeed bhai. Believe us!' I said.

'Let me tell you guys, before giving IPCC exams, the candidate must have completed nine-month articleship. How will I do that? Do you both have an answer?' asked Gorakh.

Everyone was silent.

'We will manage everything, leave it on us,' said Kairav. 'You just promise us that from now on, you will start preparing for IPCC exams. We will provide everything you need.'

'I can't do it. Why don't you understand?' shouted Gorakh.

'But you were going to do it, right? Then now, what's the problem?' I said.

'I was going to do it when I was healthy, but now I am not,' Gorakh shouted.

' Don't lose hope. If you succeed, think about how your life will change forever. Even if you are not able to do it, no one is gonna blame you, because you tried. We will always be with you bhai,' said Kairav.

'Also Gorakh, it's not just about you. It is about every person who may have gone through the same tragedy. You have a chance to become an idol for such people. Many lives will change because of your determination. You have everything that you need. Once you are successful, you can help others as well. We will not say anything more than this,' I said.

For the first time in the entire conversation, Gorakh did not respond. He was thinking deeply.

'Awesome work bhai, you did what you are best in,' whispered Kairav in my ears.

We left him alone for a while. After sometime when we entered his room, it happened; he was studying.

To solve the articleship problem, we came up with a plan. It was simple. Kairav would request one of the CA in his firm to take Gorakh for articleship. We would request him that Gorakh would do field work on two days – Monday and Saturday. For the rest of the days, he would be working from the office.

The next question was how Gorakh would do the field work. The solution was that, on Monday, Kairav would be with Gorakh for the whole day and take leave from the office in place of the holiday that he used to get on Sunday. And on Saturday, I would be with Gorakh for the whole day. The plan was accepted by all three of us.

❖

The next day, Kairav went to his office. I was in Goswami sir's lecture and was waiting for Kairav's call. The mobile vibrated and I checked my cell. It was Kairav. I was eager to hear what must have happened. I went out to take his call.

'Hello, how did it go? Give me the good news,' I said.

'Ok, listen then, I was going to talk to the CA but was unsure whether he would listen to me or not, so I didn't talk to him,' said Kairav.

'Why? It means that our plan failed,' I said.

'No you Donot, first you listen to me completely,' said Kairav. 'I was unsure, so I went to my director and told him everything. I requested him to talk to the CA and guess what, he talked to him. The CA is ready for our proposal. The director also granted me an extra holiday till Gorakh's articleship, which means I don't have to go to the office on Sunday. He told me to cover up the work in the remaining five days of the week.'

'Oh my god, what a wonderful news. I am so happy,' I said. 'By the way, what is Donot?'

'Donot means a man who is both an idiot and a donkey. Yesterday, Gorakh and I invented this word for you, how is it?'

'It's ridiculous. Bye,' I said. He was laughing and I disconnected the call.

Saturday arrived and I went with Gorakh to every place that his CA told him to go for the accounts-related work. Rajesh, the CA was a good-hearted person. He did everything he could for Gorakh.

'The day you will become a CA, I will be more proud than anyone,' Rajesh had said this to Gorakh.

❖

It was Monday and I wore my lucky shirt so that everything goes well. When I entered college, I came to know that there was a small welcome ceremony for the new students. We weren't invited to it. I was sitting in my class waiting for her.

The ceremony ended and students started coming into the class. And then, she arrived. She was wearing bluish-white jeans and a red trendy top. Her smile looked more beautiful than ever. My heart skipped a beat. I felt as if I had seen someone important to me after so many years. I was mesmerized by her beautiful eyes. Due to the rush of emotions, I fainted.

'Open your eyes,' were the words I heard when I woke up. My face was wet, due to the water that was sprinkled on it. I was lying on the bench. I was trying to stand, but felt weak. My eyes started searching for Simran. I saw her sitting on the front seat. I stood up somehow and then tried to not look at her.

'You should go home and rest,' said the lecturer.

'I am fine ma'am. I will stay,' I said. I wasn't ready to leave the college, not when I could see her. I was sitting on the last bench, looking at her. My focus on Simran got disturbed when the peon entered again with announcements.

'All the students here are informed that those who are interested in Dr Govind Lal Batta's internship should register their name in a group of four. The groups will be shortlisted depending on their proposal which should consist of the idea, the designing technique and the utility aspect.

'Later among the selected groups, Dr Govind Lal Batta will select one group. The selected group will be allowed to make a project under the guidance of the world-famous scientist. The project will be funded by him.'

There was a murmur in the class.

'He will surely select you,' said Manoj. 'He was impressed by you at the seminar.'

'I am not very keen bhai,' I said.

'There is one more announcement,' said the peon and everyone became quiet.

'The new students will be here till the next semester. The college will be dividing the students into two divisions. In this way, the new students will get to interact with the old students,' said the peon.

'Let's check your luck dude! Will she be in the same division?' said Manoj.

'Don't irritate me,' I said. Manoj left me alone. I was not the only one tensed; there were other existing couples of the class. Deep down, I was hoping to be lucky. When the list was displayed, I moved aside all the students to check my name. I saw Simran's name in division B. Excitedly, I searched for my name. It was present a few roll numbers above her name. I was also in the B division. I took a deep breath of relief. God was with me.

I turned back to go home, but I ran into Simran. She was trying to move others so that she could have a look at the notice board. I was standing in the middle of her way, looking into her eyes.

'Did you see your roll number? If yes, then please see mine as well,' she said in her melodious voice.

Without thinking much I replied, 'Your division is B, and roll number is 32.'

'I didn't tell you my name. Then, how did you know my roll number? You didn't even check the notice board,' she asked. I got trapped.

'Let's party brother, we are in the same division,' said Manoj, grabbing my shoulder and forcefully taking me from there. It was a narrow escape.

20

Back to Normal?

In college, more than half of the students came to know about my feelings for Simran, but I didn't know what she felt for me. We were in the same batch for practicals. Her magnificent smile and her long braided hair always made it difficult for me to concentrate in the class.

It had been two months and everything was going well. Gorakh's articleship and Kairav's job was going steady.

'Slowly, everything is back to normal,' said Kairav to us at the Chinese bhel corner.

'Yes, I too feel the same way. Soon, I will finish my engineering, Gorakh will become a CA and you will become the director of the company. How is that?' I mumbled.

'Becoming the director of the company will take time,' said Kairav.

'Why don't you propose to Simran?' asked Gorakh, out of nowhere.

'I don't think I love her that much,' I lied. I was afraid and shy.

'What do you mean by *that much*? You either love her or you don't. There is nothing in the middle,' said Kairav.

'Tomorrow you are going to collect your hall ticket, right? This is the perfect moment, bhai. She will be there, propose to her.'

I wanted to propose, but was scared to talk to her. Often, I asked for her notes and clarified my doubts with her. But things didn't really take off. I was competing with other boys who liked her.

'Okay guys, I have decided that I will propose to Simran tomorrow,' I announced. Everyone was very excited.

❖

The next day, I left for the college as Kairav and Gorakh went to their offices. I took my hall ticket and was waiting for Simran. She arrived, which made me very nervous. I had a rose that I was going to give her while proposing.

Finally, I saw her and she saw me. She took the hall ticket and I went near her.

'Simran, I wanted to talk to you.'

'What happened? Is it something important because I am in a hurry?'

'Yes, it's sort of important,' I said, trying to hide my nervousness.

'Can we talk somewhere less crowded?' I asked. She hesitated a bit, but then smiled.

'Fine, let's go to the class.'

She told her friends to wait in the canteen and she would be coming in a few minutes. We reached the class. The lights were dim; it was a very romantic and lovely environment.

'Say what you wanted to,' she said.

'I wanted to say that.... today's weather is awesome, isn't it?'

'Really? You could have said that down there,' she replied.

'No, wait… there is something else that I want to say. I… I like you a lot. I mean…I…I love you.' My eyes were closed.

We were quiet for some time. I looked at her finally and said, 'Waiting for your reply, it's okay if you don't love me.' It wasn't okay.

'Actually, the thing is that I already have a boyfriend. I would love to be your friend though,' she said, without looking into my eyes.

'It's okay, that's…that's good news,' I said. 'Let's go from here.'

We both came out of the class. She moved towards the lift and I said, 'I have to meet Mr Goswami. You can carry on. I will meet him and then leave.' She nodded her head in return and went inside the lift.

As she left, my tears broke all the barriers and started flowing. I wanted to stop crying, but my tears didn't listen to me. I was deeply hurt. My heart broke into a thousand pieces.

While going back home, I saw Simran in the college canteen. I tried to turn my face and walk away from there but was unable to do that. My body wasn't in my control. The conversation between Simran and her friend was a bit audible.

'He looks so boring, I knew you would never say yes to him.'

'Am I mad? He belongs to a typical middle-class family and lives in a chawl. I live in a bungalow. Don't know what he was thinking. He is also an emotional fool. I knew if I would tell him that I don't like him, he would keep on trying. So I lied about having a boyfriend. He is not my type.'

'Yes exactly, what a loser!'

I heard everything and cursed myself for stopping there. I went out of college with a broken heart. Her words echoed in my mind. Somehow I reached back home. My head was aching so I slept. Then, I woke up in the evening.

'Why didn't you wake me up, mom?'

'You were sleeping so deeply. I called you several times but you didn't wake up. I was unable to make poha at this time.'

Her jokes were just like mine, typical middle-class. I was waiting for Gorakh and Kairav on the ground. I wanted to tell them how Simran had broken my heart. I was busy thinking about Simran, but Kairav's call interrupted it. He called me urgently to the Shyamak hospital with Gorakh's parents. I found Kairav in the waiting area of the hospital.

'Bhai, what happened to Gorakh?' I asked.

'He fell today,' said Kairav. 'It's my fault, I should have taken care.'

'Tell me exactly what happened.'

'We were on the field, suddenly Gorakh's right leg got stuck in a pothole on the road. He was going to fall flat on his face, but I was in the front so he caught me. Thus, he didn't completely fall, but got hurt on both the legs,' said Kairav.

'Not your fault bhai,' I said.

'It wasn't paining earlier but then, after an hour, suddenly Gorakh was in so much pain that he wasn't able to walk. I quickly brought him here,' told Kairav.

The doctor came outside after half an hour.

'How is he? What's the problem? Is everything okay?' asked Kairav.

'I feel the pain is due to blood clotting from inside. I have given an injection, but I can tell more after examining the X-ray report.'

Gorakh was brought outside and was looking a bit relieved now. He was then taken to the X-ray room. The reports came in an hour. The doctor called Mr Verma inside, but we too followed him.

We sat in his cabin and the doctor held the X-ray in front of a light. He pointed at the end of the left leg and said, 'Can you look at this part at the end of the leg? See, there is something gathered.'

'In short, it means that Gorakh can't wear the prosthesis now on the left leg.'

'What?' I said.

'Because of the internal injuries, both his legs, especially the left one has become very weak. There is blood clotting. If the left leg is forced to move, the injury on the hip bone may increase further. His prosthesis are also hard. For avoiding all this, my suggestion is that he will have to stop walking as of now. For the right leg, he can wear a softer prothetic after a few days, but for the left leg, there is a lot of pressure applied on the hip bones for the movement. I won't suggest wearing any type of prosthesis in it.'

'He started walking only a couple of months ago. And now, you are telling him to stop walking?' said his father, his voice trembling.

'Sir, it's sad but true,' said the doctor.

'Let's go from here,' said Kairav. We came outside his cabin. Gorakh's dad looked discouraged and wasn't feeling well, so I was holding him all the time.

'He looks like a new doctor, he knows nothing. We will check with another doctor,' I said, but then, I realized that the doctor was walking behind us.

'Sorry,' I said.

'It's okay, I know you both are worried about your friend. I respect you both; you can consult other doctors if you want. I will also search and inform you if I get some information.'

We exchanged our numbers and the doctor went back to his cabin.

His inefficiency to walk was going to affect our dreams of making him a CA, which was now his dream as well.

'No one can stop my friend from being a CA. No one can stop him from walking. We will find some way. Nothing can stop us from having a wonderful future,' said Kairav.

❖

When we reached home, Gorakh asked about the injury and we told him everything.

'I am sorry Gorakh, I let you down. All this is happening because of my carelessness,' said Kairav.

Gorakh did not say anything. He was sitting for a while, and then slept on the bed and we put a blanket on him.

'Gorakh, what are you doing bhai? Talk to us, sit, we will find some way,' said Kairav, but Gorakh didn't move.

I tried to snatch his blanket, but suddenly he rose and said, 'I want to stay alone for a while. Please leave me alone. Please.'

Kairav caught my shoulder and signaled to leave. We went out of his house.

'He can't walk right, but he can work on the computer. Thus, he can continue his articleship. It's not a big deal,' I said to Kairav.

'I know, I will be talking to the CA about this, he will mostly say yes but—'

'But what bhai?

'We will never understand his pain. Only a person going through this situation can understand it. I can't see him like this. I wish I would have gone through the accident. I wish I would have died at that moment, but Gorakh wouldn't have to go through all this,' he said. His eyes became wet.

'Don't cry bhai! He will be fine. I am here with you. Don't lose hope,' I said and hugged him.

'I believe in you and us,' he replied.

Kairav talked with the CA, and it was finalized that Gorakh would be continuing the articleship. I returned to my home to study as my exams were going to start soon.

In the evening, Kairav returned with fruits and other eatables. Together, we went to see Gorakh. He was looking fine. He was ready for the articleship. He was ready for becoming what he wanted.

21

Mom is Always Right

Kairav took Gorakh to the office in a taxi every day. He had to carry the wheelchair as well because Gorakh couldn't walk. He took him everywhere in the wheelchair.

My exams were going on, so I was preparing earnestly for them. I saw Simran many times, but ignored her. I was now least interested to know anything about her. But somewhere deep in my heart, it hurt whenever I thought what she said about me.

It was my last exam. I was bored and wanted the exams to finish soon. I saw Simran again, this time with a boy. I was furious. It was more than jealousy. It was the anger of betrayal.

I finished my exam and came out of the class. Manoj came out behind me.

'What happened bro? You are very quiet these days. You don't chase Simran now?'

I told him everything as I trusted him. Manoj was my college best friend.

'Sorry to hear that, bhai. Don't worry! There are better girls out there.'

'I don't wanna talk about it,' I said.

'Cool. Anyway, are you giving your name for Mr Batta's project? If yes, then I am with you, let's try to make something together. I will be fun.'

'I am not interested Manoj.'

'I get it. See you soon. There are still two days to register the names, so if you change your mind, do inform me.'

I went home and started thinking what I would do in these holidays.

I decided to eat Chinese bhel with my friends, so I went to them.

'Yummy bhai, thank you for bringing it,' said Kairav.

'No, thank you bhai! My exams are over so I have more time now.'

'You should do some internship. It would be helpful for your placements,' said Kairav.

'I am feeling very low these days, so I am not able to focus on anything.'

'Why are you feeling low? You have stopped sharing your feelings with us,' said Gorakh.

'I still love her. When the college was open, I was able to see her, but now, I won't be able to be around her anymore.'

'Forget her bhai, she is not your type. You will soon find someone better,' said Kairav.

I was going to speak further about my feelings, but Kairav moved out as he received a call. He then came to the door and signaled me to come out.

'What happened?'

'It was the doctor's call. Remember, who had said that Gorakh can't walk. He found a solution through which Gorakh could walk. So, he has called us now.'

We left the house immediately. We were eager to meet the doctor.

'Where is Dr Dilip?' I asked the receptionist.

'In room number 113, but he is with a patient. You will have to wait.'

We waited outside, and as the patient came out, we rushed inside the room.

'How can you help him, doctor?' I asked.

'See, Gorakh's legs are injured internally. The main problem is that they are weaker to take the force required to drive the hard prosthetic legs.'

'Yes doctor, you said this earlier, now what?' I asked.

'Behave,' whispered Kairav catching my shoulder.

'So now, after searching and asking my seniors, I got the solution. The force is exerted on the legs because they move the prosthesis. To avoid this force, we have to use prosthesis that do not exert force on the legs. The prosthesis should function on its own by taking the orders from the mind.'

'You mean mind-controlled prosthesis?' I asked.

'Yes, these prosthesis catch the brain signals responsible for the foot movement and thus, make prosthetic legs work according to that.'

'Oh my god, that's awesome. From where can we get these prosthesis?' asked Kairav.

'The prosthesis that we are talking about is developed by US scientists. They are working on it, but haven't started the sales or production on demand. They are still developing it. Also, the cost of such prosthesis will be near fifty lakhs.' I stood from my chair.

'You are talking about impossible things. First of all, when the prosthesis are not yet out, how will we buy them? And, even if it is available, how will we afford it? Doctor, we belong to a middle-class family,' I shouted.

'He is right,' said Kairav. 'What kind of solution is this doctor?

'I found this while researching and wanted to share it with you guys. The rest is in your hands,' said the doctor.

We left the hospital.

❖

We decided not to tell Gorakh about our meeting with the doctor because the solution was not really feasible.

When I reached my home, I told everything to my mom.

'There must be some way beta, you should help him,' my mom said. I was shocked to hear that.

'Mom, I am a lower-middle-class boy, how can I help him?'

'You are a careless person, Raj. Right now, you think you can't do anything. That's why you are not even trying. I know you more than anyone else. You are capable of achieving the impossible,' my mom replied.

After hearing the same old dialogue that every mom says to his son, I became very angry.

'What should I do according to you? Tell me, mom. Should I force the scientist in the US to immediately launch the mind-controlled prostheses, and after that, I rob the nearest bank to get fifty lakhs? Or should I kidnap their president and inform the people that, until and unless you give the prostheses to my friend, I won't leave your president. Or I should make the prostheses for him myself?' I shouted to make sure she knows I can't do anything.

'Considering all the options, I would suggest you consider the third option. You are an engineer, after all,' she beamed.

My mom slept after that, but I didn't.

Can I do it? Is this possible? If yes, then how? These questions were dominating my mind. I searched the internet whole night about the basics of prosthesis.

But then, I realized that even if I try to make it, from where will I get the products? I will need lakhs of rupees for it. I woke up in the morning and found that I had slept on my desk.

I was still clueless about how I would be able to help Gorakh. I decided to sleep on it and think later while sitting alone in the stadium. But then I received a call. It was Manoj.

'How is the first holiday going bhai? Decided on any trips? How does Goa sound? We will find a girl for you there,' said Manoj.

'No bhai, there are things more important than trips and girls,' I said.

'Oh really?' he chuckled. 'Talking about important things, did you consider participating in the project competition?'

Oh my god! The path was in front of me and yet, I was still searching for it everywhere.

'You are an amazing guy, Manoj. Thank you so much,' I said.

'I know that but why are you saying this all of a sudden?'

'Leave it! We will be registering our name for the internship.'

'Finally,' he said taking a deep breath. 'We will have to discuss the topic soon.'

'I have decided it already. We will be making mind-controlled prosthetic limbs.'

'Sounds good! I am in. Who else will be in our group?'

'Only you and me; we don't need anyone else.'

'Not possible bro, at least four members are required.' I thought for a moment.

'Ask Gaurav, if he is in then, both of you meet me in the college at 11,' I said.

'Okay done!' he replied.

I went to Gorakh's house and called Kairav out.

'What happened bhai?' he asked.

'I have decided something very important bhai,' I said. I didn't know why I felt so confident. The memories of the time when Gorakh went with me for making my income certificate were flashing through my mind. I was determined to do something for my brother that no one else could do.

'What have you decided? Tell me,' asked Kairav, shaking my shoulder as I was lost in my thoughts.

'You remember the seminar that I hosted?'

Kairav nodded. I continued, 'Dr Batta is organising a competition where students get to work on project ideas. The winner's project will be funded by him. I have decided that I will take part in this competition where I can work on mind-controlled prosthetics. If I get selected, I will be making it for Gorakh,' I said.

'Woah. Are you serious? Amazing! That's a very good decision bhai. I am proud of you. I know you can do it,' said Kairav.

'I needed your support. Now, no one can stop me,' I said.

I went to college after taking Kairav's laptop. I was waiting for Manoj and Gaurav in the canteen.

'Hello,' said Manoj.

'Hi, both of you,' I said.

'Why are you in such a hurry about the project?' asked Gaurav.

'You guys already know that Gorakh lost both his legs in the train accident. I want to share that we would be making prosthetic legs for him,' I said. They looked at me with compassion.

'This project has not yet been done successfully by anyone else. The US scientists are still working on it. If we succeed, we will be appraised and recognized all over the world. This project can be our ladder to success,' I said. I was glad to see that my partners were as enthusiastic as I was.

'We will do it for us. We will do it for Gorakh. Isn't it Gaurav?' said Manoj.

'Yes, for sure! Gorakh is our brother as well,' said Gaurav. I looked at them and saw trust and unity. 'Raj, at least four members are required for the project. Tomorrow is the last date for registration. After that, we will have to submit the other information regarding the project in the next seven days. And then finally, there will be a presentation in Mr Batta's lab, where he will select one group for the internship,' said Manoj.

'You please do the registration and check whether only three members can participate. If not, then we will search for someone,' I said to Manoj.

❖

I returned home and soon after lunch, I started searching for the information to prepare the technical proposal. We met in college every day and remained there till late at night to make the best proposal. We knew it was not easy, but we had to do it.

The biggest issue was that the technical proposal was sent from students all over India. Our proposal needed to be unique so that it would get accepted. We kept in mind every minute detail. The sensors required to catch the signals, the material required to build the outer structure, the design, the efficiency – we kept everything in mind. We tried our level best and submitted the proposal on the submission date. The results were to be announced after a week.

We were eagerly waiting for the results. When the day came, we were thrilled.

'We are selected, congrats buddies,' said Manoj, and we hugged each other. It was our first step towards a bright future.

I finally recognized the engineer within me!

22

The Presentation

'I knew your project will be selected,' said Kairav. I was busy preparing for the presentation, so Kairav came to meet me at my house.

We didn't know if we would succeed or not, hence we decided to hide it from Gorakh. I knew if I could complete the project, it would be the best gift that he could ever get.

I was ready in my formals as it was the presentation day. It was in Mr Batta's big lab. We came to know that twenty groups from all over India had been selected. Now, we wanted to be "the one".

I went to college where Gaurav, Manoj, and a few staff members were waiting for me. The teachers told us few important tips for the presentation. We were the only group selected from our college, and thus we got lots of appreciation. The principal ordered the staff to support us in our project, but our topic was such that none of the staff had much information. We left the college and I took blessings from lord Hanuman.

❖

BLARO (Batta's Lab and Research Organization India) was a big dome-shaped building. We entered through various security systems. Cameras were everywhere. Our mobile, bags, and laptop were kept at the security counter. We only had a notebook, a pen and a pen drive with us. As we walked towards the hall, we saw various engineers and scientists working on big and small machines. It felt as if we had entered a high-tech world.

We reached the hall which had many chairs and a big stage. I had collected all the information, and Manoj and Gaurav made the PowerPoint presentation. We decided that in the presentation, Manoj would be introducing our project, Gaurav would be talking about the process, cost and implementation and I would be talking about the social significance of our project. The main thing that we were not certain about was the cost. Though we came with an estimate of twelve lakhs, it was not a small amount. On completing our research, we came to know that in the US, the cost of the mind-controlled prosthesis included the profits that the company wanted and the taxes. But our approach was completely different. We didn't want the profits. We just wanted our friend to walk.

Again, we had to give our names before entering the hall.

'Where is the fourth member?' asked the person who was taking down the names.

'Let me tell you, sir,' said Manoj. 'Raj, you see where we will be sitting.'

Gaurav and I went to find our seats. There were four seats reserved for our group. Soon, Manoj joined us.

Everybody was waiting for Mr Batta. Finally, he came on the stage and took over the mic.

'Hello, everyone. I am delighted to see many brilliant minds here. Coming to the point, I would select the group based on the relevance of that project and the passion which you demonstrate while talking about your idea.'

Our group number was 11. We were literally shivering. This was the first time we were doing something so grand.

'Group 1, topic name, Drone Security system, please come on the stage,' said the anchor. Four students stood up and plugged their pen-drive into the laptop. A big LED screen was behind the stage. One of the students started with the introduction which elaborated upon the need for surveillance. They did a fantastic job. Although, we were impressed by them, we were getting more tensed.

The group of students kept on coming and our tension went on increasing.

'Every group here is well prepared and we are lagging behind here. I am not telling this to lower your courage, I am telling this to clear the picture so that we can focus better and win the war. Any ideas?' I asked.

'I know what we have,' said Gaurav.

'Yes, you are right. Our motive for coming here is very different. It is one of a kind opportunity for us to give a new life to people like Gorakh. We have to convey our unwavering passion and commitment to our cause,' I said. I was able to feel their thoughts. At that moment we were like a single soul in three bodies.

'Group 11, topic name, Mind-Controlled Human Limb Prosthetics.' announced the anchor.

We went on the stage. After introducing our group, Manoj started telling about the materials involved and compared mind-controlled prosthesis with the ordinary ones. He talked about all its features and functions. Gaurav explained to people that it is a difficult task to assemble all such high-tech devices, sensors and mechanisms in a single product. He talked about how our cost is lesser as compared to that of US prosthesis. People clapped, but something was missing. I understood that it was necessary to make people understand the need for this project in the society. Finally, I went on the stage.

'Hello everyone, I am happy that I got this opportunity to speak before you all. I will be happier if I could make you understand the need for our project. In this universe we are never alone, we have family, friends and many other people with whom we are emotionally attached. We always want the well-being of these people.

'We are a part of a collective fraternity called humanity. Every day, all over the world, many people go through accidents and are not able to recover from it. Yes, I am talking about differently-abled people. Their inability to walk snatches their right to move freely. To overcome such difficulties, scientists came up with the idea of prostheses that help them to make their life easier. The people wearing these prostheses face many difficulties as they aren't in their control. It is difficult to walk in crowded places. With these prostheses, many times they fall and get hurt. Our project is going to bring a revolution in this field. We are going to make prostheses that can be controlled by the mind of the wearer. The difference is that our designed legs will be stronger and efficient. There is an urgent need for mind-controlled prostheses, as it is a matter of equal rights and happiness,' I said and took a deep breath.

Many people were amazed and I was trying to analyze whether I gave my best. It was soon proved by the huge applause that filled the entire hall. I was shocked to see Mr Batta standing up and clapping for me. I called Gaurav and Manoj to share the stage space with me. It was an unbelievable moment.

The other groups completed their presentations. Soon, it was result time and Mr Batta went to the stage.

'I am so amazed to hear such brilliant ideas from future India. I was pleased to hear all the group presentations. I don't want to create much suspense. So the group that is selected by getting five more marks than the runner up group number...'

Our heart was beating fast. I had never been so tensed before in my entire life. 'Group number 11.'

Upon hearing that, we started to jump and shout. I was feeling very proud. Mr Batta then called us on the stage.

He pointed towards me and said, 'This boy is such an amazing speaker. I am hearing him for the second time. He speaks from the heart. Do you want to say something Raj?' he said and handed me the mic. I was too emotional at that moment, as I was finally going to do something meaningful for my friend. Something that no one else could do for him!

Wiping my tears I said, 'Today, I am happy that our dream of "equality of efficient walking" will be achieved soon.'

Soon the program was over. We were told to come with all details of the project after two days.

❖

'Congrats bhai. I had told you that you will be selected. I went to Siddhivinayak temple to pray for you, here is the prasad,' said Kairav.

'I walked barefoot,' he added.

It reminded me of the day when he had laughed at Gorakh about going barefoot to the temple if he got good marks.

'Why don't you come to meet Gorakh now,' said Kairav.

I was quiet for a moment. I was feeling bad as I didn't give him time for more than a week.

'Don't think too much, come with me,' said Kairav and took me to Gorakh's house.

We went slowly towards Gorakh's room. I felt good as I saw him studying.

He raised his head and saw us and said, 'Oh busy guy, how come you are here sir.'

'To check whether you are studying or not,' I replied.

'Sir, you don't have to worry. I remember the little speech you gave me about studying and changing lives.'

'Stop calling me sir.'

'I am kidding bhai, don't worry! I know that there must be something important and also it's necessary to concentrate on internship. It's your final year, after all.'

'Internship… How you came to know about it?' I asked.

'I told him yesterday about your TV-making internship,' said Kairav.

'TV making internship? Oh yes, I am doing it. They teach me how to repair a TV. Is your TV working? I wanted to check how much I have learned,' I said.

'No, please don't touch my TV,' he said and we giggled.

❖

On our first working day, I got ready to go to BLARO. Upon reaching there, we were greeted by a gentleman.

'Good morning, you are welcome here!' He was wearing a white lab coat and had a tablet in his hand.

'Good morning,' we replied.

'My name is Diego Kori, and I am Mr Batta's assistant. I will be guiding you initially and will take care of the initial requirements of your project. Mr Batta is a bit busy for now, but he will be your guide soon,' said Diego.

'Hello sir, nice to meet you,' I said.

'I would have felt nicer if all four of you would be present here. Where is the fourth member?' Mr Kori asked.

'Sir, we are only three,' I replied.

'What? It's not possible. It was one of the important rules mentioned in the guidelines that the group must contain four members. Fewer or more members will not be entertained,' he shouted.

'But sir…' I was about to say something but suddenly, Manoj said, 'Sir, the fourth member is on the way.'

'It's ok. It is better that you all arrive on time together from tomorrow,' said Diego.

He went inside and told us to wait for the member.

'Why did you lie, bro? You should have said that our group has only three members,' I told Manoj.

'Calm down dude. It is of four members,' he said.

All of a sudden, we heard someone coming from the entrance.

'This is the fourth member,' grinned Manoj. Gaurav and I looked towards the door.

'Simran! She can't be our partner. I can't bear her for a moment,' I shouted after looking at her at the door. She was wearing a white shirt tucked in blue jeans. She directly came towards me.

'Why did you give my name as a member in *your* project? Is this how you want to take revenge? Let me tell you, I know how to handle middle-class people like you,' she shouted.

'Do you think you will speak rubbish and I will tolerate it? Get lost!' I replied.

She was going to catch my collar, but then Manoj caught me and took me to a corner.

'Listen, calm down! I gave her name.'

'But why? You know what she did to me bhai.'

'Yes I know! This is how we will take our revenge. Here, she is alone. You can fight with her without any fear.'

'Sounds good, but you know I can't bear her even for a moment.'

'Shut up. I know you want to bear her for your entire life. You don't have to lie to your best friend.' I blushed.

We went back and Diego also came.

'Finally, all four are here, let's go inside,' said Diego.

'Sir, I want to say something,' said Simran.

'Sir, this boy Raj, he gave my name during registration without telling me. I am not a member of the group.'

'Is that true?' he asked.

'No sir, she is lying. She begged us to keep her in the group. But afterwards, when she came to know that the project is difficult, she backed out. That's why she was absent on the presentation day also. You have the participation form, right? She had signed it. If I am lying, ask Manoj and Gaurav,' I said. They agreed with me.

'Simran, you have to do this now because you are registered. All of you follow me,' said Diego.

'I will complain to the principal,' Simran said.

'Let me tell you that it is a national project. If you will tell principal sir that you don't want to participate, he will take actions against you, not us. You can't leave now,' I said. We all laughed.

She was stunned and looked like a loser. A sense of happiness with a tinge of pain rushed through me.

23

A Small Fight

Three months passed and we were still working on the project. In the beginning, when we started working, it seemed impossible to achieve. But after a month, when Mr Batta arrived, we got the right direction. He enlightened us on the intricacies of robotics. It was always fun working with him. His vibe made us more passionate.

Watching Simran was an added delight. She used to help us but looked uninterested most of the time. She used to behave very sincerely in the presence of Mr Batta. But in his absence, the high-class girl used to show her true face. I loved fighting with her. Daily quarrels gave me a lot of thrill and energy.

I used to come to the lab at 8: 30 a.m., and then Mr Batta and I used to plan our day and start working. Others reached daily at 9:00 a.m. Sometimes, we even stayed overnight to complete the task that we had decided for the day.

Our college principal exempted us from the compulsory 75% attendance rule so that we could smoothly work on the project. We gave term test exams twice in our seventh semester, and soon placements were going to start. Everybody knew that if our project got ready, we wouldn't have to worry about the placements. So, we were not preparing for it. Our complete attention was dedicated to our project.

With Mr Batta's help, we were in touch with a prosthesis specialist. He told us that mind-controlling isn't necessary for below-knee prosthetics as they get support from the knee and cause minute difficulties to the wearer. He said that for the above-knee amputees, a mind-controlled prosthesis would be a revolution. It would take support from the waist of the wearer.

We started working on both left and right leg prosthetics for the above-knee model. We were busy making the internal parts which would be the real machinery of the prosthesis. Soon, after the completion of the mind-controlled device, we would have to build a body above it to make it look like a real leg. For the prosthesis that can fit Gorakh, I had to take the measurements of Gorakh's leg after the completion of the internal part.

Mr Batta permitted us that after the prosthesis was ready, we could give the left leg prosthetic to Gorakh. So everything was going as per the plan.

❖

One evening, while we were working in the lab, Mr Batta told us to make a power source for the legs. We had already designed the battery that we were going to use for the legs to operate. These chargeable batteries were smaller in size and lighter in weight, but they had the efficiency to work uninterruptedly for four hours. Simran took the responsibility for fitting the batteries and controlling the power. We had to use a dropping capacitor to drop the voltage before it reached the sensors.

Everything was ready and we had to start the batteries to check whether the legs start their initial functioning or not. We had designed a headphone-like device that took brain signals and gave them to the sensors of the leg. We started the battery, but before we could test it, sparks started coming out from the sensor. We shut the supply and checked the sensors. They had burnt.

'The sensor must be of poor quality,' said Simran.

'Okay, smart brains! Let's continue tomorrow. It's late. Go home,' said Mr Batta.

'Yes, let's try again tomorrow,' said Manoj. They started removing their lab coats.

'I will stay here to check the problem with the sensors. We may have to use a different type of sensor,' I said.

'I am feeling sleepy, I will see you in the morning then.' Mr Batta said and left.

I started checking the sensor. It was used after research and was verified by Mr Batta. So, I was shocked that it didn't work.

On checking, I saw that the capacitor was also burnt. The burning of the capacitor showed that the sensor was not faulty, but it happened because of overpowering. Simran did the selection of the dropping capacitor and its connection.

When I had a closer look at the capacitor, I found that it was of a lower value than needed. I realized that it was not a mistake, but done intentionally. I immediately removed the lab coat so that I could catch her outside and ask her about this. Luckily, she came into the cabin.

'I forgot my hair clip,' she said.

'Oh, there it is!' She picked up the clip kept on the table and started going out.

'Why have you done this?' I asked.

'What?' she asked quizzically.

'I know you intentionally connected the wrong capacitor so that the sensor would burn.'

'Have you lost your mind? You know that the sensor was faulty.'

'I know you are at fault and not the sensor.'

'Believe me.'

'Shut up, you bitch! Don't try to fool me,' I shouted. And then the expressions of her face changed. The sweet innocent face turned devilish.

'Be in your limits! Yes, I have done that. But how will you prove it?' she said with a wicked smile.

'I have the burnt capacitor, and it is enough to prove your intentions.'

'Where is the capacitor?'

I tried finding the capacitor as I had kept it on the table.

'Here it is,' she said, showing me the capacitor in her hand, and smirked.

I ran towards her to snatch the capacitor. We were both fighting in the cabin. I caught her from behind and was trying to open her fist to take the capacitor. She turned towards my side and pushed me back. I ran towards her but then, she hit me between my legs with her knee. I fell. The pain was unbearable.

'You bitch,' I said slowly as I was unable to shout.

'You idiot, never mess with me again,' she said and walked towards the door.

I stood up and caught her hair. I pulled it and she shouted in pain, 'Please leave it.'

'You should have thought this before hitting me,' I said and pulled it more.

'Ahhhhhh,' she cried. Tears rolled down her beautiful eyes. I felt her pain in my heart and I left her hair. She wiped her tears.

'Never show me your face again. You don't want to be in the project, right? I will tell everything to Mr Batta. You will be free from tomorrow. Get lost!' I said.

'I don't want to see your face, you moron,' she said and left the cabin.

I didn't know why her tears made me cry as well. I was ashamed that I fought with her and hurt her. I was unable to work, so I went home. I called Manoj and Gaurav and told them that Simran was responsible for the burning of the sensors.

❖

I woke up in the morning with the firm determination that I would tell Mr Batta everything about Simran. If she wanted to go, I wouldn't hold her back. My project was much bigger than my revenge.

I reached BLARO at 8:30 a.m.

'Hello Raj, you are so punctual, son. I know you will be a very successful man one day,' said Mr Batta.

He made it more difficult for me to speak.

'What happened? You look tense,' he asked, patting my back.

'Sir, I wanted to confess something.' I closed my eyes and said, 'Sir, I made a mistake.'

'What mistake, son?' he asked.

'Sir I—' I was going to speak but then, Simran came and interrupted me by saying, 'Sir he wants to say that yesterday, the sensors burned because of the capacitor. It was my mistake, I used the wrong capacitor. I am sorry.'

'Wait what? So you made the mistake? Then, why is he apologising?'

'He said that he is the team captain, so he should take the responsibility,' said Simran.

'Oh Raj, you are such a good leader. It's okay, mistakes happen. Simran, be careful next time,' said Mr Batta and went to receive a call.

'Why did you not let me free you from the project? If you are thinking that you will create problems again, then you are wrong. I am going to tell him everything,' I said and walked towards Mr Batta.

'Stop, Raj!' said Manoj.

'Thank god, Manoj. You are here. You don't know what she did just now.'

'I know everything brother. Now listen to me, she is with us now. At night when you told me what happened between you and Simran, I called her. I told her that I gave her name while registering and not you. I told her our real motto behind the project. After listening to the truth, she was feeling guilty for what she did. She has decided to rectify her mistake by helping us,' said Manoj.

'You really want to help now?' I asked her.

She held her ears and said, 'I am so sorry for ruining the project. When Manoj told me your purpose for creating this project, I understood your anger. I felt guilty. From now, this project is mine too. We are now a true group.'

Then, she came near me and whispered, 'By the way, I didn't apologize for hitting you. It's perfectly justified because you pulled my hair.'

I gave her an angry look and got a beautiful smile in return.

24

The Clip Thief

It is easier to work with a group where the members are chasing the same goal. I was in such a group. My fight with Simran continued, but it did not affect our project.

Our seventh semester was over, and we were in the middle of holidays. The most important thing was that Gorakh's IPCC exams had started. He was well prepared and we knew it, but the tension never left us.

'He will pass for sure,' said Kairav, sipping coffee. We were sitting outside the exam center and Gorakh was giving the exam inside.

'I know that, teddy. I am worried about my project.'

'What happened? You were saying that it will be complete soon.'

'Yes, it will be completed bhai. We are just facing a problem with the proper movement of the legs. We are thinking about it and will soon find some way. We have taken three days off to think,' I said.

'Shut up, I know you are missing her,' Kairav said as he saw Simran's hair clip in my hand. I had got it while pulling her hair. It was now my lucky charm.

'Is she my girlfriend that I will miss her?' I said hiding my face.

'Donot, you think I don't understand anything? Don't forget that I am your senior in this department,' he said proudly.

'Get lost,' I said, and he went to talk to Sapna. I loved Simran, but I knew I was not of her status. We weren't meant to be.

People came out of the center, and then, a man brought Gorakh out on the wheelchair.

'How was the exam?' I asked, taking the handle of the wheelchair in my hand.

'It was easier than I thought,' said Gorakh.

'Today, the party is from Gorakh's side. All his papers went well,' said Kairav, coming in front of the wheelchair.

'Oh hero, once I will become a CA, then I will give a party. At present, I have nothing to give you both,' said Gorakh.

'You are talking like me, bhai. By the way, your friendship is enough for us,' I said.

Gorakh started preparing for CA finals as he was sure that he would crack IPCC.

❖

Three days passed and we were back in BLARO with the same clueless faces.

'Soon, our last semester will start and we still haven't completed the project,' said Manoj.

'We all know this. Think about what we don't know,' said Simran.

'Okay, you guys think, I will be back in an hour,' said Mr Batta and left the cabin.

'We are going to return our books of the last semester; we will be thinking about the project outside,' Gaurav said and left.

I was unknowingly looking at Simran while thinking why the prosthetic legs were not moving in the desired direction.

'Stop staring at me,' she said in her cute angry style.

'I am not interested in you,' I said.

'You are a liar and a thief,' she smirked.

'Mind your tongue, miss. What have I done?' I asked.

'Don't act smart! I know you stole my hair clips.'

I got scared that she will ask me to give back the lucky charm, so I said, 'No, I didn't.'

'See, I told you, you are a liar. I saw the clip in your compass box.'

'I want my clip back,' she said, and the thing happened that I was afraid of.

'It's not your clip, is your name written on it? I won't give it back,' I said.

'So sweet. It means you don't like me, but are interested in my things.' She blushed.

I got mesmerized just by looking at her. For the first time, she blushed too. I was thinking whether she liked me as well.

'You still love me, right?' she asked coming closer to me, looking straight into my eyes.

'No,' I said and closed my eyes for a moment. My heartbeat raised.

'I don't have any boyfriend. I lied that day,' she said.

'I know you lied. I heard you talking to your friend saying I am not your type. I belong to a typical middle-class family living in a chawl and you live in your bungalow.'

'I am sorry for that Raj. I didn't know much about you back then. I was showing off.'

'Still clueless engineers?' said Mr Batta, interrupting us. A beautiful moment was destroyed.

'You both should also leave for today then,' said Mr Batta.

We agreed. I knew Simran wanted to talk more.

'Raj, I want you to come with me to a tech conference,' said Mr Batta.

'Come, we will go in my bulletproof car. See you tomorrow Simran,' he said and walked towards his room.

The wound of the day she rejected me and the things she had said were fresh again. I looked back and saw her sad. She was waving her hands. I waved back.

❖

The next day, Mr Batta called us early in BLARO.

'As you all are unable to think how you will fix the movement issue, I am giving you some other task. Do this first, and then start thinking about the main problem,' said Mr Batta. He looked disappointed.

'The task is to design the outer body of the leg as well as the internal design of the hollow part in which Gorakh's actual legs will be inserted so that he can wear this prosthesis.'

I had already taken Gorakh's left leg measurements. We started working on the task. I was consciously maintaining distance from Simran and talked to her only when it was necessary. Whenever she came near me, I walked away, pretending my work was over at that place. I continued it till evening.

Mr Batta came to check our work and said that we could leave for the day. Manoj and Gaurav got ready to leave. I told them I was going to stay back to complete some work.

'I will also be working here tonight,' said Simran.

Everyone was surprised as this was the first time she was going to work overnight.

'Simran, it's ok, you can continue. Your family will be worried.'

'I have already asked my father about it. He permitted me,' said Simran and Mr Batta allowed her.

We were working, and Mr Batta was in the cabin till 10:00 p.m. As he left the lab, Simran came near me and asked, 'Why are you ignoring me today? Why are you not staring at me?'

'Why should I stare at you? I am not your lover,' I replied.

'Oh really, then look into my eyes and say that you don't love me,' she said. I saw desperation in her eyes.

'I will not do all this,' I said and started working.

She was silent and I got worried. I turned my face to see what she was doing. I ran towards her, as she was crying standing near the door. I locked the door from inside and wiped her tears.

I held her face with my hands and said, 'I love you, Simran. Please don't cry.'

Her sad face immediately turned into a mesmerising blushing face.

'See, I was saying that you love me. I love you too, Raj.'

We hugged each other tightly.

'I was waiting for this hug since the first time I saw you. You will not understand how much I love you,' I said. She looked at me and again leaned on my chest.

'So tell me, are you ready to live with a typical middle-class boy?' I asked her.

'Stop teasing me,' she said. 'I am ready to live with you anywhere. I just know that I love you very much.'

We came closer, and her lips met mine. We kept on kissing and removed the lab coat that we were wearing. She was more passionate than me. There were no boundaries. I started kissing her neck and then moved a bit lower. She pushed me and said, 'This is not our bedroom. Let us go to the restroom.'

We immediately locked the cabin and rushed towards the four-bed restroom, though we needed only one bed. I immediately closed the door and pushed her towards it. We kept on kissing. I started unbuttoning her shirt. I was kissing on her soft tummy and moved a bit upwards to have a different feeling. Soon, I picked her and placed her on the bed.

Removing anything that came between us, we did everything that we wanted to do. That night was the loveliest.

25

A Surprise

In Raj's voice

It was not new for us to wait for the results. IPCC results were going to be announced, and so we were eagerly waiting for it.

'Hey look, the page has loaded,' said Gorakh. He was trying to open the result page, but it wasn't loading earlier.

He entered his seat number and I prayed to lord Hanuman.

'Passed,' said Gorakh, and Kairav started dancing.

'It's not only me brothers, but it's also us who have passed today,' said Gorakh with teary eyes.

I informed Simran, Manoj, Gaurav, and Mr Batta about Gorakh. They were very happy. I thanked god for giving people like them in my life.

I returned in the evening from BLARO to meet Gorakh. He was studying. His enthusiasm towards cracking CA exams increased a lot in these months. That's why he chose not to rest for even a single day.

'Hello, You are studying more than me these days,' I said sitting on his bed.

'I guess my articleship will complete before your internship,' he asked. 'It's taking too long, isn't it?'

I was unable to answer him.

Suddenly Kairav came there and said, 'Leave it donot. Engineers are not paid very high anymore. Our CA will rock. If you do ten more internships, then also your salary will be lower than ours.' They both giggled.

What Kairav said was sad but true. I was worried for my future. We didn't even attend the college placements. Our project was our only ray of hope. We had completed its body, but the movement mismatch was still an issue.

We were in the lab with Mr Batta. Gaurav was testing the prosthesis since the morning. We had a dummy body on which we put on these mind-controlled legs.

Then, one member of our team wore the controlling headphones. When we walked, the dummy body should have walked, according to our theory. But in practice, the motion of the dummy body didn't match ours. When we moved our left leg, sometimes the right moved and sometimes, the left leg. Mr Batta was confused about the problem.

'There is some small error, but what is it?' said Mr Batta, scratching his head. Manoj and Gaurav used to do the testing most of the time. I decided to try once. I asked for the headphone from Gaurav.

The same problem existed when I tried. There was a coordination problem. I stopped testing the legs and got tensed. I was afraid that our hard work would get wasted if this wasn't fixed.

I asked for a glass of water. Simran rushed to bring her water bottle, which she never shared with anyone. I smiled and raised my right hand to take the bottle, but then I noticed that when I moved my right hand, the right leg of the dummy body moved.

I gave back the bottle in her hand and then moved my left hand and saw that there was some movement in the left leg. I tested for some time and understood the problem. I called everyone.

'I think I know what the real problem is, and got its solution as well,' I said with a broad smile. Everybody was shocked and happy to hear it. Many other scientists including Mr Batta were present in the cabin.

'Tell us, Raj,' said Mr Batta.

'Ok, sir. We worked for a long time and almost completed our project, but we faced a single problem, which was coordination. After having a close look, I realized the problem. The sensor in this control headphone that we used for sensing the signals from the brain for walking is catching the legs movement signal, along with the hand movement signal. To understand clearly, let's think about what happens when we walk.

'Normally when our left leg is in the front, at the same time, the right hand comes in front. This happens with all of us. Therefore, due to this unwanted dual signal catching, whenever we tried to move the left or the right leg, there was some unwanted motion in right and left leg as well,' I said and tried to make everyone understand the real problem.

'Then what's the solution according to you,' asked one of the engineers standing among the crowd.

'The solution is very easy; we have to separate the two signals and then, ground or suppress the hand movement signals,' I replied.

'Amazing son! Brilliant,' said Mr Batta.

Everyone started clapping for me and I saw the happiness in Mr Batta's eyes.

'Let's get over with this then,' said Mr Batta. 'Few more hours to go.'

It was a late night but none of us went home. We were busy achieving our target. Finally, we did it and I wore the headphones for the final testing.

When I moved my left leg forward, the left leg of the dummy moved. When I moved my right leg, the right leg of the dummy moved. We supported the upper fake body with a loose harness and tried the walk.

Eureka! It was successful. I felt like I was doing the most important walk of my life.

'You people don't know what change you have brought in the world today,' said Mr Batta. 'This is huge.'

We tested the prosthesis the whole night. Thinking about Gorakh wearing it and walking gave me chills. It was 5:00 a.m., and someone knocked on the cabin door. Gaurav opened the door, and it was Mr Batta.

'Have you all ever been in a press conference?' he asked us.

'No sir,' we replied.

'Well, today you have to be present in one,' said Mr Batta. Mr Batta had told about the success of our project to every important person he knew. He called the media to let the world know what we had done.

I ran towards the entrance of BLARO to take my cellphone and called Kairav.

'Hello, teddy. We have done it bhai. The legs are ready,' I said and a tear of happiness touched my cheek. I was never so happy. I opened my arms to feel the air. I closed my eyes. I was flying. I had never felt so relieved in my life.

Finally, I had done something for my friend, for my brother.

'Oh my god. You don't know what have you done bhai. I will immediately inform Gorakh about this.I will tell him that he will get his legs back today. I am proud of you, bhai,' said Kairav.

I knew that Kairav was as happy as I was, but I wanted to surprise Gorakh in the evening, so I told Kairav to keep this a secret.

'Don't worry, I will not tell him anything and will not let him watch your press conference also. I will hide his mobile as well. Bhai, please try to come as soon as possible. I am dying to see Gorakh walking,' said Kairav.

I heard his voice breaking. I understood his pain. Seeing Gorakh in a wheelchair always saddened us. Gorakh never cried or shared how he felt, but we knew what he was going through.

We all went home to get ready for the conference. Mr Batta had told us that every news channel was going to show the news because it was an achievement. All four of us reached the lab to verify the working of the prosthesis.

The press conference was in the BLARO premises itself. Soon, reporters from various news channels started coming. Seating arrangements were ready. We were going to show them the live demo of the working of the mind-controlled prosthesis.

'First of all, I would like to tell you that we are gathered here today to let the world know that we have made the first mind-controlled prosthesis which can be immediately brought into practice. And, the second thing is that it is made by my young students who are sharing the stage with me. They came up with the idea and executed everything. I provided them with the basic information that they needed and the resources. I would love it if you all appreciate their work,' said Mr Batta, and everyone was surprised to hear that.

Everybody clapped for us.

'Let's start the session,' said Mr Batta, and the reporters started asking questions from us. We answered every question as we knew every aspect of it.

Someone then asked us, 'Who came up with the idea of the mind-controlled prosthesis among all of you?'

As the question finished, everyone on the stage looked at me. The reporter understood that it was my idea,and she said, 'Speak sir. Tell us the motivation behind it.'

'When I realized the pain of the people who cannot walk, I was very sad and wanted to do something to eradicate this pain. The next question is, how did I realize their pain? I have a friend, actually, I should say my brother. His name is Gorakh. One day, he met with an accident and lost his legs. I understood the pain when I saw what my friend was going through. My mom is the person who germinated the seed of this idea, and today, we have made it. The problem is not only with my friend, but it is also with many of our brothers and sisters. Thus, to eradicate their problem, to give them the "Right To Walk", we all worked together in this direction.'

The press conference and the demo were finally over. We were again sitting in our cabin and thinking about what to do further, along with Mr Batta.

'I have already talked to the officers and started the paperwork for patenting our technology. What are you guys thinking now?' said Mr Batta.

'Sir, I am thinking about how to surprise Gorakh. I want all of you to come with me. You have played a huge role in my journey, which is why we will be able to see Gorakh walk again,' I said.

Everybody was excited to join. We left the cabin along with the left leg prosthesis and one of the controller headphones. The right leg prosthesis and the extra controller were left in BLARO.

As promised, everybody was happy to give the prosthesis to Gorakh. They were the true gems my life gave me. We were in Mr Batta's car. He told his driver to make us reach safely with the prosthesis.

I called Kairav to know about the arrangements made there.

'Hello, we are coming with the prosthesis. Gorakh still knows nothing, right?' I said.

'Yes come, we are ready here. Gorakh is studying in his room, and I didn't allow anyone from the locality to inform him. Also I removed the cable wire so that he can't watch TV and hid his phone,' said Kairav and giggled.

❖

At the locality, Manoj and I were holding the prosthesis. As people saw us, they began to gather. I saw many faces after quite a few months as I was rarely present in the locality.

'Congrats man. Amazing work. Son, you have made our locality proud. We saw the news. You guys are true heros,' said an uncle. We entered my house.

I kept the prosthesis and hugged my mom for being so supportive. The prosthesis was kept in my room.

Suddenly Kairav came and hugged me tightly. He lifted me up and moved around multiple times. I started feeling dizzy.

'You are a true genius bhai,' he said and I saw contentment in his eyes.

'You go and bring Gorakh, I have a few arrangements to do here,' said Kairav. I didn't know how he'd react, but I agreed.

I went to his house and saw his parents outside.

Mr Mehta rushed to hug me. I was able to see tears of happiness in his eyes. Gorakh's mom was very emotional too. She came near me, lowered my head, and kissed my forehead. She said, 'If I had another son, I am sure even he would not have done the things you did for him. I wish that everyone should have a friend like you and Kairav.'

'We are your sons aunty, and Gorakh is our brother. Now you both go to my house. I will bring Gorakh there,' I said and they left.

I slowly entered his room and saw Gorakh lying on his bed with his eyes open. The room's lights were off. As he saw me, he rose turned on the lights.

'Hello, how come you are here now? It is your internship time, right?' he said.

'You looked tensed, bhai. What are you thinking?' I asked him.

'Why will I be tensed?'

'Then what were you doing with lights off?' I asked. He went silent.

'Please say whatever you have in mind,' I said, sitting near him. I kept my hand on his shoulder.

'I was thinking about my last race that I won from you,' he said and smiled. He easily hid his pain behind his smile.

'Well friend, it's the time you should receive the prize for that victory,' I said.

'I don't understand,' he said.

'You will understand everything soon,' I said and made him sit on the wheelchair. I locked the door after taking him out and moved towards my house.

'Where are we going?' asked Gorakh.

'To take your prize!'

Hundreds of people were standing outside my house. As they saw us coming, they cleared the way for us.

'Why are they here? Tell me,' said Gorakh. 'Are they fencing the ground?'

'No. Patience,' I whispered in his ears. As we entered inside, I saw Simran and others standing on one side of the room, and on the other side, the TV was on. It was the repeat telecast of the morning press conference.

'Raj, you are on TV!' said Gorakh, and then he started listening to the news.

'It was Kairav's idea,' whispered Simran.

Gorakh heard everything and then he turned back the wheelchair to face me.

'Here is your prize, bhai. You have to win many more races from now,' I said.

'Is it true?' Gorakh asked looking at me.

'Yes, it is true, and here it is,' said Kairav pointing towards the prosthesis kept on the bed.

'Donot,' said Gorakh with tearful eyes.

'Come here guys,' said Gorakh with open arms. Kairav, Gorakh and I hugged each other.

Few reporters barged into my house to take pictures and interview. Gorakh wasn't interested in giving interviews, so the reporters took some pictures of us and left. I told Gorakh about Simran, Gaurav and Manoj, who were equally responsible for the making of the prosthesis.

He thanked them wholeheartedly. After looking at Simran he whispered to me, 'Is she the same high-class girl?'

'Yes, but now she is my girlfriend.' I smiled.

Everything was done. Gaurav, Manoj and Simran were leaving. I went outside to drop them.

'When will we meet now?' asked Simran making a puppy face.

'Tomorrow in the college,' I said and was going to kiss her but realized that my mom was present there.

They left and I went inside. I explained to everyone how the prosthesis would work. Kairav had bought a softer prothesis for Gorakh's right leg. We decided to start the practice the next day, but Gorakh was impatient. We were impatient too. We started the practice that night itself.

Gorakh wore the controlling headphone and the prosthesis.

'It is so soft, fit and comfortable. It's magical,' said Gorakh. 'I can't thank you both, but I want to thank god for giving me friends like you.'

26

The Lucky One

In Gorakh's voice

The day I would never forget was when Raj, Kairav and others surprised me.

After a long time, I understood that god does play games with our lives, but it depends on us whether we lose or win.

Though it was a mind-controlled prosthesis, it took me months to be a perfect walker. The controlling headphone was later replaced by a controlling cap. Raj and his friends showed it as their major project for the final year. They received prizes and certificates from their college. Even the chief minister honoured them in a program arranged especially for them. They became famous for their work.

Soon, I started walking like before or I should say, better than before. They were my legs. If used continuously, the left leg and the cap needed to be charged every four hours. I felt better than before. We had never thought this day would come. I used to go out alone without any fear.

Kairav became assistant director in his firm, and Raj passed engineering and got a job. We were sitting in a hotel, as Raj had thrown a party. Raj and Simran were working in an IT firm as it paid a higher salary than any other electronic company. Simran and Sapna met for the first time at the party. They looked beautiful. I was happy for my friends. I had decided that I would not marry. I wanted to stay single.

'Order whatever you all want to. Today is the day you have both been waiting for since your birth, right? Raj will give a big party. See, I reached above Chinese bhel,' he said to me and Kairav.

'Everything has improved, but you are still a donot,' said Kairav.

'Hey, what's a donot?' asked Simran.

'Should I tell her?' I asked Raj.

'No, guys. I am giving the party, and you all are making fun of me. I will not talk to anyone,' said Raj, acting sad.

'Ok…Ok we will not tell her about Bindiya as well,' said Kairav.

'Now who is Bindiya? Raj, you tell me who is she?' fumed Simran.

'We are kidding Simran, don't worry,' I said.

It was a nice dinner. We discussed the mess we had made at Marine Drive and how Kairav met Sapna after that. We all enjoyed it very much. I saw that Raj-Simran and Kairav-Sapna needed some space, so I decided to leave them alone. I knew they wouldn't let me go, so I told them that the charge of the leg is 40% and I needed to charge it.

'But you charged them before coming,' said Raj.

'I guess I forgot to turn on the switch,' I said.

'And you call me a donot,' said Raj. 'Wait, we are also coming.'

'No bhai, it's ok. I will catch you at home,' I said. 'I want to rest as well, so I will be leaving for now.' I left from there.

❖

I was a bit sad while walking. The road was empty and the cool breeze made me feel lonelier than I was.

Walking alone was not fun. I was thinking what my life would have been if that accident hadn't happened. Would I have studied with this passion? Would Raj have done something that would have made him so successful?

I knew the answer. A big no!

I realized that everything is connected in this world. Everything happens for a reason. We never know what will happen to us after a defining moment.

I was thinking at that moment and found myself very lucky.

Who has a friend like Kairav and Raj? Who invents something for you? I had heard stories about people whose relatives didn't care about them after such events.

I was lucky. Then, I saw a man who didn't have his left leg above the knee, but he wasn't wearing any prosthesis. He was walking using a crutch. I saw the difficulty he was facing in walking. He tried to cross the road and his crutch slipped. He fell flat on the road. I saw a car coming towards him, but it stopped on time. The man tried to get up, but was unable to. He was hurt and taking a long time to get up.

The man inside the car shouted at him, 'Get up quickly, dumbass.'

I became very angry. Firstly, I helped the man to get up, and then I scolded the man in the car, 'Can't you see he is specially-abled? Don't behave like an animal.'

'If he has a problem, he should walk on the footpath. Why is he crossing the road? Move aside, I am in a hurry,' said the man in the car and left from there.

I brought the uncle near the footpath, and we sat on a public chair. I saw his face. He looked old and poor.

'I was crossing the road because the municipality school, in which my son studies, is on the other side.'

'It's fine uncle,' I said. The man looked at my face for a few seconds and then, said, 'You are Gorakh, right?'

'Yes uncle, but how do you know my name?' I was shocked.

'Are you kidding? Ask any specially-abled person in India, or I should say the world. They are talking about you. You are very lucky. We all are happy for you, but it hurts to see how we are discriminated against,' said the man.

I did not know what to say to him.

'I have heard that government jobs are there for people like us,' I said.

'Beta, you didn't face what we faced. We moved from one place to another to search for jobs. We stood in lines for hours. They told us to give online exams. I am illiterate, how will I crack their exam? Can illiterates not be specially-abled? There are various schemes, but not everyone is able to enjoy the benefits. Even many educated specially-abled people are suffering. In such conditions, how will we survive in this world!' he cried like a child.

I was able to see the pain he must have gone through. I was able to see that he was speaking the truth.

'What do you do uncle?'

'I polish shoes on the railway station,' he said. He saw that I was sad and quickly wiped his tears with his stained dhoti.

'Leave all this, beta. I am happy for you. Be successful and happy. Make all of us proud!'

I offered him some money, but he refused. We all are humans, and we all have the "right to walk". I decided that I can't be so selfish, and I had to do something for others like me.

❖

I went home but felt restless. I immediately needed to do something for such people.

Kairav and Raj came together to my home in the morning. They looked quite happy as they entered my room.

'I want to talk about something important,' I said.

'We have something more important to tell you, bhai,' said Kairav and stopped me from speaking.

'Do you know as I was coming here, a call came on my phone,' said Raj.

'So what, listen, I want to say something urgently,' I said.

'The call was from the office of India's biggest businessman, Mr Rakesh Chand. He is currently the richest person in India,' said Raj.

'What did they say?' I said.

'The person on the phone said that Mr Chand wants to buy our patents for the leg. What do you think? How much did he offer?' Raj asked me.

'No, I don't have any idea,' I said.

'Ten crores!' both of them said together.

'Ten crores. Is this true? Am I dreaming? Pinch me, someone,' I said. Then Raj showed me the spot on his hand where Kairav had pinched him a moment ago.

'You are going to be so rich, Raj. You will be getting ten crores man,' said Kairav. 'We will call you Raj Sethji from today.'

'No bhai, I will be distributing it to five people, my group and Mr Batta. So I will get two crores only,' said Raj. Hearing the amount, the thought of helping people left my mind. Raj informed other members about the deal, and everyone agreed. Mr Batta wasn't interested in money, so he said to distribute it among the four members.

❖

The meeting was fixed for the next date. Raj and his project partners, along with Kairav, went for the meeting. I was waiting to know the outcome. They reached back home with the papers that they had got from Mr Chand's office. They had to read, sign and give it back the next day. Raj started reading the points given in the paper.

'After signing this paper, Mr Raj, Gaurav, Manoj, and Mrs Simran will have no rights on the technique of building the product, and neither they can get involved in any such activity in the future. Chand Group of Enterprises will have complete right to do whatever they want with the technique,' read Raj.

Coming out of the dilemma, and after hearing the points, I got worried. I didn't want the chance of helping people go in the hands of people that I didn't trust.

'I have a different opinion, if you all agree to listen,' I said.

'Yeah Gorakh, go ahead,' said Raj.

'The mind control prosthesis that you all invented was for me as I was unable to walk. But I am not alone in the world who is facing this problem. Mr Vikram Chand is buying the patent so that he can earn money out of it. You all have made it in twelve lakhs, so Mr Vikram will sell them at a higher rate. He is a businessman. How will poor people get access to it? If you all let the project remain in your hand, then you can decide the price. Then,we can work in the direction of making it accessible to poor people as well. Once you sign the document, your dream of "Right to Walk" will never come true,' I said.

'I guess he is right,' said Kairav.

'Are you both serious? From where will the money come for the initial building of the legs? It involves huge funds as well as a huge workforce, to complete the demands on time. How will you pay them because we won't earn from poor people? And what if your complete idea fails,' said Manoj.

Manoj was right. Everybody got lost in thinking.

'Who all think Gorakh is right? Raise your hands,' said Raj, breaking the long silence. Raj, Kairav, Simran and I raised our hands.

'We know a huge cost will be required for your idea, Gorakh. Also, getting 2.5 crores is not a small thing for us. Still, I would say that if you can arrange an amount that is sufficient for building at least 6-7 prostheses, we both are in. We don't have a single penny to invest in this,' said Manoj.

'Sorry guys, but if we can't arrange the amount till tomorrow or think of a better idea, then we will sign and give this to Mr Chand. This is a once in lifetime opportunity. I hope you understand what we are thinking,' said Gaurav.

They both left the house.

'They are right. This is a dream come true! 2.5 crores isn't a small amount! We are thinking for the betterment, but do not have the potential to achieve it right now. I guess you both will also have to take the same decision ultimately,' said Kairav.

'Yes. Why should you leave such a glorious opportunity?' I said with a deep pain in my heart.

27

Calm Before the Storm

In Raj's voice

I never thought in my life that I would be earning 2.5 crores at once. When I heard it, I started thinking about the things I will do with that money. But what Gorakh said was also right. I proposed the right of every human to walk freely in my speeches. So how could I let my dream fall in some unknown hands, just for money?

We were thinking about how we can arrange the money. I asked my mom for some suggestions, but she was in favour of taking the 2.5 crores.

We thought for the whole night, but didn't get any solution. It was 5:00 a.m. and we felt sleepy, but we wanted some breakthrough.

'Sleep for a few hours at least,' I told them.

'I guess you are right,' said Kairav and slept on the sofa.

We were sleeping peacefully, but our sleep got disrupted by the ring on Kairav's mobile.

'It's an unknown number,' said Kairav and picked up the call.

'I am coming immediately,' said Kairav.

He sounded very angry, so I got worried. I woke up and saw his face which was red with anger.

'What happened Kairav? Whose call was that?'

'It was the police. They have caught Robert. Let's go immediately. They caught him while he was stealing in someone's house. They are bringing him to the police station. Let's go. I want to kill that rascal.' He was furious and punched the wall.

I was furious too, but handling Kairav was more important at that moment.

'Are you coming or not, I am leaving,' said Kairav and opened the door.

I took my mobile and informed my mom. Then, I ran after him. I called Gorakh and told him to meet us outside.

We took a rickshaw and reached the police station. Robert was not yet there as we reached earlier than the police. We were waiting outside.

After a few minutes, the police van came and they took out a man. He had a fair complexion, many healed scars on his face, and was completely bald. It was Robert. As the police took him out, Kairav rushed towards him and punched him in the face. He fell to the ground.

Then, Kairav started hitting him with his legs.

'Rascal, you didn't feel pain while killing a lady. You son of a bitch! I will kill you,' shouted Kairav.

I, along with two constables, pulled Kairav back. As soon as Robert stood up, I punched him so hard that his teeth broke.

'You ruined the lives of both of my friends. I wish I could kill you, bastard,' I shouted.

'I will kill you,' shouted Robert, looking at me. The police officer slapped him.

'What is wrong with you guys?' said the officer and pushed us back. 'You guys, please control. We have a special officer to handle him.' They took Robert inside and we went with them.

Robert looked like he hadn't eaten any food and his clothes were also torn. Gorakh too arrived and sat near Kairav. He kept his hand on his shoulder.

We wanted to be with Kairav to keep him composed. We were worried that he might do something wrong if we would leave him alone for a moment. One hour passed, and we were still waiting for the special officers.

I checked my mobile and saw that there were eight missed calls of Gaurav and Manoj. I went outside to call Manoj.

'What happened Manoj?' I asked.

'Bhai, did you get some solution?'

'No.'

'Ok, then meet us, let's go to Mr Chand's office for signing the document.'

I went inside and told Gorakh about this.

'We have no other option left, bhai. Also, today is the last day to accept the offer. Do as your friends are saying; at least they will be happy. I am here with Kairav. Come back soon,' said Gorakh.

I did not want to leave them in such a critical condition, but the deal was important for others, so I had to leave. I told Gorakh to call me whenever needed.

❖

Soon, I went home, took the papers and reached the headquarters of Chand Enterprises.

'Wait outside. Sir is in a meeting,' said the peon standing outside.

After an hour, we were called inside.

'Hello, scholars. Glad to meet you all. What's your decision then?' said a person sitting on the chair.

'You aren't Mr Chand,' said Manoj.

'No, obviously not! Mr Chand has gone for a ten billion dollar deal in the US. I am Nilesh Viroppa,' said the man. 'Mr Chand does have eyes on this deal as well. So what's your decision?'

'You thought Mr Chand will be there for a ten crore rupees deal?' I whispered and started calculating the value of 10 billion dollars in rupees.

'Sir, we are ready for the contract,' said Manoj.

'I knew you all will be ready that's why I made your cheques ready as well,' he said and signalled to his PA. The lady handed over to us the cheque of 2.5 crores each.

'I have a meeting now, so please quickly give me the signed papers,' said Mr Viroppa. We knew his time was more valuable than ours. Three of them signed the papers, and it was my turn. My hand was shaking, but I had to do it. Suddenly my phone rang, I ignored it, but it rang again.

'Sorry, I have to take this call,' I said.

'Whaaat? Are you sure? Oh my god!' I shouted.

'What happened, Raj?' asked Simran. I quickly collected the cheques from their hands and tore them.

'What are you doing, idiot?' said Manoj.

'What is this? What are you doing?' shouted Nilesh.

'Sorry, we aren't interested in your deal,' I said. 'Let's go guys.'

'You already signed the deal, you can't back out now,' said Nilesh.

'They signed it, I didn't, so it's useless,' I replied.

'What are you saying Raj? Sign it, we still have the chance,' said Gaurav.

'Yes, sign it. I will give fresh cheques of 3 crores to each of you,' said Nilesh.

'Nope, not interested. Sorry for the inconvenience,' I said. I caught Simran's hand and walked out of the office building.

'You don't understand what you have done. He was giving us 3 crores.' shouted Gaurav as he came out.

'I know what I have done. Trust me, let us go to my house. I will explain everything there,' I said.

We reached home in a taxi. I told them to sit on the sofa and offered water to drink. But they weren't interested in anything.

'We got the money,' I said all of a sudden.

'What? How?' asked Simran.

'For that, we have to go five years back,' I said. I told them about Kairav's mom's kidnapping, the breaking of our friendship, Gorakh's accident, and Kairav's return.

'Oh my god. Kairav is an amazing friend. But how it is related to the money?' asked Manoj.

'The kidnapper who killed Kairav's mom is Robert. He got caught today. The other kidnapper who got caught previously is Prince. Prince had told the police that Robert stabbed Kairav's mom and dad and then ran away with the money. He had lied.

When police interrogated Robert, they came to know that Robert had stabbed Kairav's parents, but the money was with Prince. He was busy hiding the money and till then, Robert had escaped. Prince thought that he would come back and take the money if he didn't get caught.

Today, when the police found the truth and twisted Prince a little, he accepted that he had hidden the money and shared the location. When police searched the place, they found the three crore rupees. Kairav told me that he wants to invest in our idea. He wants to be part of it,' I said.

'Wow, amazing. It seems that god is with us,' said Simran.

❖

We kept a meeting at BLARO. The meeting consisted of seven people including Mr Batta, the three of us, Simran, Gaurav and Manoj. We had kept the meeting to decide how we would start.

'First of all, we need to know the number of people interested in our product,' said Manoj.

'I have the solution. We have to create our website and start online registration for the people interested in the world's best prosthesis. I will create the website,' said Gaurav. 'I have done an internship in website creation and management.'

'That's an amazing idea Gaurav, but how will people come to know that we are doing something like this?' I asked.

'Simple. One more press conference, leave that on me,' said Mr Batta.

'The next thing is meeting with the right people and dealing with them. I will do that for now,' said Simran.

'But we will require a place where we will work and build things. We will need an office and a lab,' I said.

'I was thinking about this. My home is empty; we can temporarily use it as a lab and an office,' said Mr Batta.

'Sir, we can't use your home. You are already doing so much for us. We will think about something else,' I said.

'My life's aim is to help people with technology. My home has been empty for years. I will feel great if it can be used for something like this,' said Mr Batta.

'Sir, you are a true legend,' I said, saluting him.

'I will be bringing the types of equipment and materials required for the making of the prosthesis,' said Kairav.

'I will be managing the finance and accounts of our company,' said Gorakh.

'I will make the prosthesis with Manoj and Gaurav,' I said.

'We will require more people if we are building a company. As our company goes big, more and more workers will be required,' said Gorakh.

'I have already decided what to do. We will conduct an interview for selecting people who are interested to work with us. The selection criteria will be based on the technical knowledge and their dedication to serve specially-abled people,' I said.

'Are we ready?' I said loudly.

'Yes, we are,' shouted everyone.

'What will be the name of our company?' asked Manoj.

'"Right to walk" something?' said Simran.

'I got it "Right to walk corporation India". How is it?' said Gaurav. Everybody loved the name.

'We will need a CEO and MD for the corporation,' said Manoj. 'I think Raj will be perfect.'

'Raj will be perfect as a CEO,' said Mr Batta.

'If you guys want, I can be a CEO for namesake. We all are equally important in this. I think Kairav would be perfect for MD position, because he already has some experience,' I said.

Everyone was clear about their responsibilities.

We decided to have the conference after two days. Our current target was to make the official website, clean the closed house and then, transform it into a lab with a small office.

Soon, the press conference day came.

'We are starting the company named 'Right to walk corporation India'. Online registration will happen for the people who are willing to get the mind-controlled prosthesis. Initially, we will start working on a first-registered-first-serve basis. The cost and other information are mentioned on the website.'

The news spread like wildfire. We started receiving many calls on the given number.

'129 registrations. We got a great response guys,' said Gaurav, sitting in our lab.

I was happy with the registrations but realized that soon, we will require more people for work.

'We have to start the interviews from tomorrow. Selected people will be given fifteen days of training. We would require professional experts from the field of prosthesis for taking measurements of the patients, for the initial exercise and training of the specially-abled, and other important processes. We will require people for paperwork, record maintenance, and back-office jobs. Thus, jobs for different posts are available from our side,' I said.

We started the interviews and training. When we made a single prosthesis, it had cost 12 lakhs. It involved the mistakes we had done. Now, when we were going to prepare the prosthesis in bulk, so less amount was required.

Thus, the estimated cost came down to 10 lakhs, but we sold it for 14 lakhs.

One year later

Gorakh became a Chartered Accountant. Kairav and I were thrilled. Our dreams of seeing Gorakh walk as well as become a CA were achieved.

We completed the making of 100 prosthesis and started working on the other 100 prosthesis with the help of the engineers we had hired. The registration count was 790 and counting. Kairav was working on opening three more branches of our company in Delhi, Kolkata and Chennai. Our target was to open our centers in the entire country as well as overseas. More than half of the registrations were from abroad.

For achieving our goal to serve specially-abled people, we requested the government, trusts, and other businessmen to support us. We received tax exemptions from the government and continued donations from many businessmen including Mr Vikram Chand. We donated half of our earnings for our mission every year. The estimated cost of the prosthesis for poor people reduced to less than a lakh.

Three years later

We had 15 branches in various foreign countries including the US, England and China, and 10 branches in India. We were looking for 20 more branches in the next two years. Just like India, we tied up with the governments, businessmen, and trusts in foreign countries to help the poor people.

Kairav and I had decided that we will not marry until Gorakh also found someone.

Our life changed. We were living in bungalows. People changed with time, but Kairav never did. Kairav still lived with Gorakh in his bungalow.

Our dream "Right to walk" was successful and then we shifted our focus to work for people without hands. We started our research in that field.

'I will drive,' said Gorakh. We were going to Siddhivinayak temple to thank god for giving us a fulfilling life where we could serve so many people. While returning from the temple, Kairav and Gorakh seemed tense and were very quiet.

I wasn't aware that our serene life was going to face a storm soon.

28

The Storm

In Kairav's voice

'Open the door,' shouted Raj, continuously knocking on the door. 'Open it!'

We rushed to the door and opened it. We knew why he was here. It was raining heavily.

'You could have rung the doorbell,' said Gorakh. 'You are wet. Why didn't you bring the umbrella?'

'I did ring the bell, but it broke on the eleventh time,' said Raj. 'Tell me why you both did it? I felt that something is wrong since we were returning from the temple and now this.'

'Come inside,' said Gorakh. I handed him the towel, and we sat in the hall. I told Gorakh's parents and my dad to go back to sleep.

'Answer me,' shouted Raj wiping his hair and face with the towel. 'Why did both of you send the resignation email to me? Why do you want to resign?'

'You know it, Raj. We can't run away from fate,' I said.

'Can you be a little bit clearer?' said Raj.

'We can't be with you bhai, and thus we resigned,' said Gorakh. 'We don't want something bad to happen to you.

We tried to make you understand this earlier, but you didn't listen.'

'Oh, now I get it, now I understand. It's again about that Panditji's prophecy. Nothing will happen to me, guys. If something had to happen, it would have happened by now,' said Raj.

'We saw the Panditji again today,' said Gorakh. 'We told him everything. He checked our kundli and confirmed that our dosh is over, but it's still on you. He said that your *rahu kaal* has started, and this can be the worst time for you. He told us to be away from you, to keep you safe'

'I swear I will kill that pandit,' shouted Raj. 'But what is wrong with you both? We work for science, and you believe in superstitions?'

'We don't care, bhai,' I said. 'We are not taking any chance. Consider that resignation final. This is our last meeting.'

'You are right, my rahu kaal has started. I can already see the effects as my friends are leaving me,' said Raj.

'It's as hard for us, but we have to do it. You should leave now. Please go out of my house, and don't try to contact us,' said Gorakh.

He wasn't looking towards Raj. He couldn't say such harsh words, looking him in the eyes.

'Are you seriously doing this?' Raj shouted with teary eyes but we didn't respond. He smashed his mobile on the floor and stormed away in the heavy rain. I locked the door from inside.

'Did we do the right thing?' said Gorakh, hiding his tears.

'Yeah, we did,' I said and we walked towards our rooms.

When we came out of the temple, I saw that panditji again. He had a big office now, and people were standing in a queue to meet him. Gorakh saw him too. We remembered his predictions about us and how they had come true. Dropping Raj at his home, we went back to him, and then, he warned us to stay away from Raj. I knew that today none of us were going to sleep.

❖

It was 2:00 a.m., and I was looking at our old pictures from Matheran. A call interrupted my nostalgia. It was Inspector Martand Pasare.

'Hello, Kairav sir,' said Martand.

'Yes, Martand sir, what happened?'

'There is bad news. Robert has escaped from prison two hours back. So stay alert. We are looking for him and have sent two constables to your bungalow as well for safety because he might come there.'

'He escaped two hours back, and you are informing me now?'

'We came to know just now, sir. He was in some other jail. Also, inform the same to your friend Raj. I tried calling him, but it didn't connect.'

I ran towards Gorakh's room and told him everything. We checked the security and everything was fine at our place.

'Call Raj,' said Gorakh. 'I am so worried.'

'He broke his phone, remember? He is not reachable. His parents are out of town. Wait, I am calling his security guard,' I said and called him, but he didn't pick up the call.

'He is not picking up. We have to go to Raj's,' I said.

'Let's go immediately, bhai,' said Gorakh. We told the armed guards to be alert and our parents to keep calm. I called Martand to send constables to Raj's bungalow as well. He lived half a kilometer away from us. We drove to his house.

As we reached the entrance, we were shocked to see the security guards lying unconscious at the gate.

'What the fuck!' said Gorakh. 'He is here. Let's go inside. Hope Raj is safe.'

'We have to be careful. Let's take the wooden stick of the guards. It seems that Robert took their guns with him,' I said.

'It's happening. What panditji had said is happening. God, please keep Raj safe,' said Gorakh.

'Don't panic, Gorakh. Stay alert. Let's go inside,' I said. I messaged Martand that Robert was here. We reached near the door of the bungalow. It was open. We tiptoed inside, but there was no one. And suddenly, we heard some noise coming from Raj's room. We ran towards it.

As I opened the door, I saw the nightmare. Raj was sitting on his knees with blood all over his face as if he had been punched many times, and Robert had his gun pointed at Raj's head.

'Welcome, my dear Kairav. Thank you for coming here yourself. I was going to visit you after I was done with him,' said Robert and laughed like a maniac.

'Listen, Robert, leave him! If you hurt him, then your punishment will increase. I know you don't want to do this,' said Gorakh.

'Punishment? Do I look like someone who is afraid of punishments? I will kill him and everyone,' he shouted.

'Raj has nothing to do with all this. It started with my family. If you have to do something, do with me. Leave him. I beg you, please,' I requested.

'Do you know Kairav, I stabbed your mom twenty times, I counted it. I made sure that she was dead. I didn't kill her because the police came. I killed her because I wanted to. In fact, I would have killed your dad as well if the police hadn't come. Damn, I got only one chance to stab him,' said Robert. My blood boiled, and I had only one thought now. I wanted to kill him. I tried to run towards him, but Gorakh grabbed my hands and didn't let me go.

'What happened? Where is the person who was begging a few moments ago?' He laughed again, louder than before. Now, we were able to hear the police siren.

'Oh, the police is also here. Let me get over with this. Let me end this last chapter of your story on a bloody note. Let me kill all of you.'

'Gorakh, Kairav, you are the best friends anyone can ever ask for. Thank you for this journey,' said Raj, a mixture of blood and tears dripping from his face.

'I will shoot on the count of three, one...' said Robert. Gorakh and I threw our sticks towards him and ran to save Raj.

Raj had closed his eyes and was prepared to leave this world. We were still far from him.

'Two and three,' said Robert and pulled the trigger.

'No…no no no!' cried Gorakh. 'No.' The trigger was pulled, and destiny played its card. Raj was lying on the floor.

'What? What just happened? Why didn't the bullet come out from the fucking gun?' said Robert scratching his head. He tried again, but nothing happened.

By that time, we reached him, and I snatched away the gun. Gorakh hit him in his stomach and he fell. I picked up the stick and started hitting him with it. Gorakh picked up Raj and put him on the bed and called an ambulance. Raj was unconscious.

I picked up Robert's gun to shoot him dead, but Gorakh caught me from behind. The police also reached there, and they took the gun from my hand. They tried taking Robert with them, but I caught his shirt and was not letting him go.

'Leave him, Kairav. We have to take Raj to the hospital,' shouted Gorakh. I realized my friend needed me, so I left Robert.

❖

We were in the ambulance with Raj. I thanked god for saving him. The gun was fully loaded, yet the bullet somehow got jammed inside. Gorakh caught one of Raj's hands and was crying. Suddenly, Raj became conscious.

'I am alive or I am in heaven with you two,' he joked.

'Stop joking, bhai,' said Gorakh wiping his tears. We told him what happened.

'You guys saved me,' said Raj.

'You didn't hear properly? The bullet got jammed. We didn't do anything. God saved you. You were lucky,' said Gorakh.

'Yes, I am lucky, and you both are my luck. We are not harmful for each other. If anything, we are lucky for each other. Remember what Robert said, as the police came, he was unable to kill Singh uncle. That means Gorakh's call saved your dad, Kairav. I remember that the three of us met on Gorakh's accident day, but what if our meeting saved him from dying in that accident.

'Why do we always think pessimistically? Because of Kairav, I got admission to the engineering college, and because of Gorakh, we made the prosthesis and gained so much in life. And today, a fully loaded gun didn't shoot the bullet even after the trigger was pulled. Everything I have and everything I will have in the future, I owe it to you guys. Please never break our friendship,' said Raj.

The heavy rainfall finally stopped and the storm ended.

Epilogue

In Gorakh's voice

A month passed since Robert's attack. He was now serving life imprisonment. We were sitting in a café.

I was happy for Raj and Kairav and enjoying my single life. Work and research for hand prosthetics were going strong. Somewhere, I felt that they were not moving ahead in their lives because of me. But I knew that they were smart enough to take their decisions.

'Gorakh, what are you thinking?' asked Simran.

'I was thinking about what we should order,' I said.

'Raj already gave the orders,' said Sapna. 'Gorakh, tell me one thing, did you ever fall in love?'

'From where does this question arrive?' I asked.

'No baba, I am just asking,' replied Sapna.

'Not love, but I liked someone. Later on, she left.'

'You never told us, Gorakh. Whom did you like? Where did she go?' asked Raj, the curious one.

'I had a thing for Mitali.'

'Your Physical Trainer?'

'Yes, Raj. I liked when she was around. I always waited for her to come and train me. But once I knew all the exercises and started walking on my own, she stopped coming.'

'Are you in touch with her?' asked Kairav.

'No bhai, I didn't dare to talk to her afterward. I felt that why would she be interested in talking to me? I can't even walk properly.'

'You never shared this with us,' said Raj. 'You always were and are special in your own way. And, everything has changed now. You can talk with her now.'

'Guys, check the third table from our left,' said Kairav. We quickly checked it out. A beautiful girl in a black saree was sitting alone.

'That's Mitali, everyone! Oh my god, what a coincidence?' chuckled Raj.

'Gorakh, go and talk to her,' said Simran.

'Are you insane? I am not going anywhere,' I said, trying to hide my blushing face behind the menu card.

'You have to go Gorakh. This is a great chance. Go talk to her,' said Kairav, lowering the menu card.

'You have to do it for us,' said Raj. 'Please.'

'What if she is waiting for someone?' I said.

'You will know once you talk to her. Go now, or I will call her here,' said Kairav.

'You guys are impossible. I am going,' I said. I prayed to god to help me.

'Hey, Mitali. How are you?' I said.

'Hey, Gorakh. Long time no see. You are a celebrity now. Sit..sit,' she said.

'Are you here with someone?' I asked.

'No yaar. I was just passing by and suddenly felt like having a coffee. What about you?'

'Same!' I said and messaged Raj to take everyone out of the café.